MW01420120

BARRACUDA

A JACK WHITFIELD THRILLER

Book 1

JOHN W. MEFFORD

BARRACUDA

Third edition.

Sugar Hill Publishing

ISBN: 979-8-876528-14-8

Interior book design by
Bob Houston eBook Formatting

To stay updated on John's latest releases, visit:
JohnWMefford.com

The Story Behind Jack

To me, Jack has always felt like an iconic name. That is likely born from my relationship with my late grandfather. A large man with a larger-than-life personality, "Jack" Whitfield was kind-hearted, the life of the party, and a bit grumpy if he had a bad day on the golf course (which usually meant one of his buddies won some money from him).

"Ga-ga" once danced with Jackie Kennedy, allowed me to drive a car by myself at the age of ten, and cooked the most amazing southern breakfast. More importantly, for decades he helped countless people from both sides of the track get jobs in the state of Tennessee. He also was a big fan of the after-dinner ice cream cone and could hit a wicked blind hook with his five-wood on the dogleg-left sixth hole at Carnton Country Club just outside of Nashville.

He had a profound impact on so many people, but none more so than this grandson, his namesake. When he passed away—I was only sixteen at the time—I was shocked to see hundreds of people show up to his funeral, including Minnie Pearl, a famous comedian from the Grand Ole Opry.

I made a vow as a teen that I would someday name a son after him. And I did. While the Jack Whitfield in this thriller series shares a few traits with my memorable grandfather and son, no one can replace Ga-ga. And no person, fictional or otherwise, can match the character or heart of my son, Jack. How he got that way is anyone's guess, but I certainly won the lottery when he entered my life.

So, while the name "Jack" might have turned trendy in recent years, I can honestly say that I know Jack better than just about anyone.

And now it's time you got to know him. I hope you enjoy the new Jack Whitfield Thrillers.

"The opportunity to secure ourselves against defeat lies in our own hands, but the opportunity of defeating the enemy is provided by the enemy himself."

~ Sun Tzu, Chinese strategist

"He who has a why to live for, can bear almost any how."

~ Friedrich Nietzsche, German philosopher

1

Donelson, Tennessee

A yawn escaped my mouth, and I accidentally dropped my keys on the darkened front porch. "Can't see a damn thing," I muttered, running my hand along the wood planks. It took a couple of seconds to register, but when it did, I smiled. "Your lovely wife expects *you* to turn on the porch lights."

After more than sixteen hours of poring through spreadsheets and dealing with grumpy clients, I couldn't wait to put up my feet, eat some home-cooked spaghetti, and let Anna massage my shoulders—but only after I tiptoed into Maddie's room and gave her a kiss goodnight.

"I get the not-so-subtle message," I called out to Anna as I closed the door. I paused, waiting to hear her playful snicker.

No laughter, no reply of any kind. Not even the sound of soft jazz music. And no garlic marinara wafting in the air.

"Anna?"

My voice quivered just slightly—my mind sensing an imbalance in the world—as I started up the steps.

"Hey, are you reading to Maddie? Let me join you." My throat turned bone dry the moment my foot hit the landing. No response from Anna. No talking or giggles from Maddie's room. I hurried into our bedroom. The bathroom light was on. A hairbrush sat on the counter. But no Anna.

My heart in my throat, I dashed into Maddie's room. "Maddie?" I flipped on the light. Covers thrown back on her bed. Stuffed animals on the floor. Empty.

I tore down the staircase, giving a quick glance at the living room—empty—then into the kitchen. A red streak smeared the tiled floor just beyond the island. Bile kicked into my throat as I dove to the floor. "Anna, Maddie!"

Only more blood and a stem from a broken wine glass.

"What in the—?"

Unable to breathe or even produce a tear, I startled when my phone dinged with a text. A desperate wish for this to be some kind of hallucination made me look at the screen. A text.

We have your wife and daughter. Leave your house and get into the black car waiting for you outside. Do it now or they will die.

2

I staggered toward the black Suburban in front of our home and slid into the back seat. The man behind the wheel demanded my wallet, keys, and phone. Incensed, I lunged for his neck, but a nearly invisible glass separator blocked my attack. The kidnappers had apparently anticipated such a response.

"Where's Anna and Maddie?" I shouted.

"Your things. Put them in the tray in the middle console."

"I'm not doing a damn thing until you tell me where you have my wife and daughter."

The engine purred, but the driver said nothing.

"Did you fucking hear me? Tell me where you took them!" I palmed the glass separator, my face pressed against it.

The driver's head turned slightly. "You heard the terms. And I would comply. Quickly."

My gut churned like hot magma. "What do you mean?"

"Put your things in the console," he repeated, monotone.

I threw my belongings into the small compartment. "Done.

Now tell me what's going on. Where have you taken my family?"

"There's a hood on the seat next to you. Put it on and cinch it under your chin."

I merely glanced at the hood before I went back to the glass partition and whacked my fist against it. "Not doing it. Do you have a ransom? Are they hurt? I swear to God, if you hurt them…" I clawed my nails into the seat.

"If you don't put on the hood, then we will sit here until the cops show up and you are charged with the abduction and murder of your wife and daughter. When they dig into your lives, they'll also find that you abused them both."

"That's a lie!"

"But the evidence will show otherwise."

"Why are you doing this?"

No response.

"Listen to me, goddammit!"

Still nothing.

I exploded, punching the glass, kicking the glass, spitting on the glass, and screaming until my voice cracked. None of it had an impact on the glass or the man.

Panting, my knuckles bloodied, I looked through the red-streaked glass. "This is fucking insane! I didn't kill anyone! What have you done?"

"Do you want to be charged with murder, or do you want to get your family back?"

"How do I know you even have them?"

"Put on the hood or go down as a killer." The driver checked his phone. "You've got twenty seconds to make up your mind."

Every muscle in my body clenched. I thrashed and shouted a string of obscenities, unable to control my rage. My terror.

"Ten seconds."

I put on the hood.

***

We traveled for hours, not stopping once. During one instance when horns honked and the driver slammed the brakes, I stole a quick peek from under the hood. A sign to Atlanta. That's when I started to count to sixty. I made thirty-two round trips to sixty until the Suburban stopped and the engine shut off. The driver opened his door, and I snuck one more furtive glance. A small, one-story home surrounded by a large canopy of trees. No sign of people, other homes, or cars.

That was my last view of the outside world until I was ushered to the Atlanta airport four days later. But it was the parting words from the driver that gave me something to chew on.

"You listen, you do what they say, and you'll live to see your wife and daughter," he said, his grip tight on my arm as he led me to the door.

"Who took my wife and daughter?"

No reply. I wasn't really expecting one, only grasping for some hope, some oxygen.

"Please. I need to know."

More silence.

I withheld the urge to lash out, and instead, took another tack. "What will I be asked to do?"

"Above my paygrade. But when Simon talks, you listen. Or else."

"Simon. What's his last name?"

"Who said it's one person?"

"Who are they? What do they want with me?"

He shoved me into the house, and the front door closed automatically behind me.

3

South China Sea

The stench of death lingered in the stagnant, humid air, penetrating every pore of her skin.

Pulling her knees tight against her chest, Cai Chen bit her lip until she'd punctured a hole. But the metallic taste of her own blood did little to distract her from the overwhelming scene before her.

She opened her teary eyes. The man who had just beaten another young girl so badly she had to be carried out of the ship's hold stood silently, a warped smile splitting his face. That wasn't the worst of his transgressions. Not by a long shot. She had overheard the name his colleagues called him: Mogwai. A monster or demon in the Chinese culture. The moniker fit him perfectly. He was the one who levied punishment against any of the girls who even hinted at rebelling.

Cai's sights fell to Mogwai's sweaty T-shirt. The frayed,

gray fabric was coated with a thick film of grease. Droplets of blood were splattered across the front at various angles, a sickening reminder of the number of beatings he had doled out during the twenty-plus hours Cai and the others had been chained to the hull of the cargo ship.

Metal clinked, and Cai held her breath. Mogwai moved into a shaft of light and yanked the chains off the wrists and ankles of another lifeless girl. She had been so pretty at the start of their journey. Her creamy complexion like that of a model. Her lustrous black hair framing her face just so, naturally. Even though every girl knew peril loomed, she'd maintained her composure, stepping with the pride and grace of a ballerina.

Mogwai leaned down, grabbed a fistful of mangled hair, snapped the girl's neck back, and angled her beaten, bloated face toward Cai. He tapped the side of the girl's cheek. "You want to look like her?" he asked in Cantonese.

Cai had forgotten to breathe. She released the air trapped in her lungs, and it came out in fluttering gasps.

"Talk. Do you want to look like her?"

She started to turn her head away.

"Look at her!"

Cai looked away, but in her peripheral vision, she could still see his psychotic glare, his snarl with chipped teeth and blackened gums.

He wasn't just warning Cai to avoid the same defiant path as the dead girl. He was inviting her, almost begging her, to cross the line so he could inflict another wave of torment.

"No." Tears bubbled at the corners of her swollen eyes, fearing she would soon be his next victim.

Mogwai released the pretty girl, and she crumpled to the floor. He walked toward Cai.

She tried to ignore him, but his leering presence would not be denied. He cracked his knuckles and chuckled like a depraved animal. He would have his way with her and discard her like she was a spoiled sack of rice.

He yanked at her upper arm, his enormous fingers nearly cutting off the flow of blood to her thin limb. She turned and clamped her jaw around his wrist. He howled, reared back, and launched a meaty right hand into the side of her face. It knocked her senseless, tiny motes of lights flickering in front of her eyes as her head slammed against the metal floor. He hauled her body upright, and she winced, waiting for the worst of it.

The door opened, followed by hard-soled shoes banging against the floor.

"What the hell are you doing? We have a shipment to deliver. The merchandise has value, even the girls. You keep killing the girls, we lose money."

The newcomer, who spoke with a British or Australian accent, was taller than Mogwai. His hair was cut stylishly, and he wore white snakeskin cowboy boots. "I will not put up with this, Mogwai." He swatted his hand toward two men behind him, barking out orders, but Mogwai didn't release his grip on Cai.

"Let her go. Now."

Cai could hear the click of a pistol loading a round into its chamber. Mogwai turned to see the barrel of the gun six inches from his nose. The tendons in his neck tensed. He didn't move.

"Now," the man in the snakeskin boots said.

Mogwai sneered. Seconds ticked by. He released his grip, and Cai fell to the floor, her legs like rubber. He shuffled backward until he disappeared through the door.

"Thank you, sir." Cai slowly pushed herself up.

The man crouched down and cupped her chin. "So very beautiful. Like a flower."

She tried to smile but could only nod, and her whole body trembled. Tired. Weak. Frightened. Angry.

"You will bring top price when we reach port."

She dropped her eyes. Her torture had only been delayed to another place and time.

The man stood and addressed the two dozen girls in the hold.

"You will all receive food, a shower, and a new set of clothes. And then when we dock, it will be time for your new adventure."

Dimples formed on the clean-shaven man's face as pitiful whimpers bounced around the space.

Cai wept silently, wondering if death at the hands of Mogwai would have been the better option.

4

Unknown location near Atlanta, Georgia

Just inside the front door of the small home, a cell phone sat on the floor with a sticky note telling me to use it.

"A mission objective?" I blinked twice at the term used in the text. And then I read further. They wanted me to travel to Macau, China, and rescue one girl, Cai Chen, from a trafficking operation. Their leverage for me to complete this mission was the lives of my wife and daughter. That was made crystal clear.

All instructions were sent over that cell phone through encrypted text messages or video tutorials.

Before I could question any of it, I was instructed to walk into a room where I had to strip off my clothes and dye my hair. Once in workout attire, I was educated on the identity I'd be using for this mission, a "legend" of sorts. When not learning about the new me, I was forced to go through brutal workouts for hours at a time, mostly sit-ups, push-ups, and chin-ups…to the tune of thousands of reps. My body trembled from overuse. The most grueling workouts since my All-American days running track at the University of Tennessee. But the mental impact was even more debilitating. I was in some type of no-man's land. Unable to fight back against nothing more than a voice. Unable to rely on resources like the police or FBI to help locate my wife and daughter. Unable to grieve.

During my transformation from Jack Whitfield to Clayton Fishbeck, my new identity, I had no direct contact with anyone. I spent most of my time in a single square room, with no idea if it was day or night. All windows were boarded up. My actions were monitored every second by cameras I could see and probably a few I couldn't. I thought about Anna and Maddie constantly, and it was impossible not to envision the worst. They'd been killed. And Simon would kill me next, whether or not I successfully completed this mission.

Flailing, at least mentally, I diverted my thoughts to try to determine how I could gain an upper hand, to learn more information. Finally, during one set of sit-ups, I concluded they saw me as a valued commodity. In what way exactly, I wasn't sure. Still, it was leverage that I could use to my advantage. The timing would have to be perfect, with me at the precipice of carrying out their perilous mission.

On my last day, I was told to put on a suit they had selected for me. Once I was dressed, interior doors opened, and an electronic voice told me to walk outside and get into the car. I walked to the front door but stopped before opening it.

Now was the time.

"I'm not going anywhere until you tell me who you are." I faced the camera positioned in the corner.

Silence.

"You need me. Tell me who you are."

The air conditioner hummed, but other than that…nothing.

"You think I'm fucking joking? You took the only people that matter to me. Tell me who you are!" Flames of rage roared through me.

"Who we are is of no concern to you," the voice said.

"Why did you choose me?" Sweat drained down my face, my torso quivering. "I'm no one special, just a guy who owns a small CPA firm in a nothing town in Middle Tennessee. Why?"

More silence.

"Why did you take my wife and child? Why not just hire me to help you, for God's sake?"

A single beat of silence, then, "We did not have the time to negotiate. In fact, you might have declined our request. We made the appropriate decision that would force immediate action. This isn't personal."

That response blew my head back. "Not personal? You stole my family! My daughter is only five years old! What the fuck are you talking about?" Spit flew from my mouth as I leered at the camera, my heart thumping my chest like a herd of wild horses.

"It is not personal for *us*. We know it is personal for *you*. That is why we selected you, Jack."

I blinked repeatedly as those words sunk in. "You chose me because I love my family?"

No response.

"Tell me! I can't do this for you—I won't do this for you—unless you tell me."

"Jack, you have the unique skill set of a world-class athlete. The agility, the focus, the strength and flexibility, the competitive heart. You have done incredible things. And we know that you will use those skills to keep that sweet family of yours safe and intact."

"What? That's your justification for kidnapping my wife and child? Because I made the Olympic team?"

"Secondly, and of equal importance, we know you'll cross

that ethical line when it benefits you."

I got still. "What the hell are you talking about?"

"Your experience with the mob boss. The cooking of the books. You recall that, don't you, Jack?"

Oxygen flooded my brain, and I reached for the wall to keep my balance. "How the hell do you know so much about my life?"

The front door to the home opened, and Simon relayed one final message. "Succeed, and you will be reunited with your wife and daughter. Fail, and you will never see your family again."

5

Over the Black Sea

A slate-gray ocean churned with white caps thirty-thousand feet below my seat on the Airbus 350, but that was nothing compared to the storm brewing inside me.

The rain and gusty winds had started some time over Romania, according to the British pilot. With our plane now rimming the Black Sea, his most recent update said we'd break through the bad weather as we approached Turkey. I peered through the window, searching for the lights of Istanbul, but saw only ominous flashes of lightning.

"Are you from Turkey?"

It took a moment for the question to register. I turned to face the woman who wore a religious habit, brown and white. She was older with a kind face. It looked nothing like Anna's, but it still sent tiny shockwaves into my body.

"The UK," I said, not looking for a conversation.

"Can you believe the hijacking at Heathrow four days ago? So thankful no one was hurt."

Four days ago. When my life was hit with a thunderous body blow. "Yes, very thankful."

"God was watching over His children on that day."

What about my daughter?

Loud conversations in different languages broke out around us, and the nun went back to reading her Bible, offering me a respite from my new persona. I tapped the screen of my four-day-old phone. Part of me prayed for any new evidence that Anna and Maddie were alive and well. The other part of me dreaded interacting with this pure evil.

There were no messages.

I caught my reflection in the darkened phone screen and touched my sideburns. A far cry from my normal sandy hair and clean-cut face, my locks and matching goatee were now platinum blonde. I looked every bit of my thirty-six years.

I replayed the mission directive one more time: rescue one girl, Cai Chen, from a human -trafficking operation in Macau, my destination. My mind instantly short-circuited, and I rubbed my temple. Not until four days ago had "Jack Whitfield" and "mission" been uttered in the same breath.

I chewed on a straw, my mind reeling with questions. Why would Simon—this unknown, shadowy organization that was threatening to kill my wife and child—want to *save* a life? Cai Chen. Someone within the Simon universe had to know her. A relative, maybe. Wouldn't they have more resources to pull off this rescue than me? Unless…

They knew of the danger and wanted to send in another party, someone disposable. Me.

I lifted my eyes—a man with a nose ring two rows up was looking right at me. Without another thought, I flew out of my seat and got in his face. "Who are you? Are you one of them?

Where's my wife and daughter?"

His eyes drew together.

I took hold of his shirt and pulled him halfway out of this seat. "If you want to live, you better tell me. Now!"

He spoke rapidly in German.

"What are you saying? I can't understand—"

A tug on my arm. I turned to see the nun.

"This man is confused by your outburst. He is going to visit his ill mother in Hong Kong."

I released the man's shirt.

"Are you okay?" she asked.

"Fine."

I dropped into my seat, out of breath. Searching for some type of emotional anchor, I forced myself to look out the window. A few lights sprinkled the darkness below.

Maddie loves sparkling lights.

Within seconds, I was stewing again about why Simon had selected me to run point on their mission. Even though I lived a mostly anonymous life in Donelson, Tennessee, at one point in my life I was considered a world-class athlete. A proud member of the University of Tennessee track team, my event of choice was the decathlon. I competed in meets across the world, where track and field was far more popular than in the states. I even qualified for the Olympics, although a pulled hamstring forced me to sit and watch. Was it possible that I'd crossed paths with one of these Simon assholes during those days? It was hard to imagine, but it was also difficult to dismiss. As was their reference to the mob boss I'd encountered in my first job out of college, before I'd opened my small accounting firm in Donelson.

As much as it gnawed at my gut, Simon was correct: I'd cooked the books for the mobster—mostly because he said I'd go down with him if I didn't. Anna and I were about to get married.

I had to put it behind me. I was left with no other option.

The owners of the firm had long ago closed their doors and retired. No way they could be part of this Simon cult. Anyone else from the dark side?

I thought about my "troubled years" as a teen. I got caught up with the wrong crowd and had a few run-ins with the law—when they caught me. Drug possession, petty theft, a few fights. Nothing major. Living with my heavy-handed grandmother hadn't been easy.

And in college, I'd dealt with a dangerous addiction to painkillers.

I'd made my fair share of bad decisions—who hadn't growing up?—and I've lived through some remarkable experiences, but of all the people I'd encountered, no one stood out as a possible Simon candidate. Not even close.

My phone dinged with a text. I looked at the screen. A picture of Anna and Maddie sitting on the floor. Maddie, scrunched up with her favorite stuffed animal Woofies, was laying across her mother's lap. Their faces were the most beautiful things I'd ever seen.

"Is that a cut?" I blew up the picture and brought the phone closer. I spotted not just one but multiple cuts on Anna's face and neck. "Maddie too?" A jagged line of blood on my daughter's chin.

My arm began to shake. I grasped the phone with both hands, but I couldn't squelch the tremors. My chest began to shake as a fury took hold of every piece of my body, spreading like a raging fire.

I punched the seat in front of me, then leaned forward, seething.

And my heart split open once again.

6

Unknown location

As a damp chill set in, Anna wrapped her arm around her daughter, Maddie, and pulled her closer.

"Are you still cold, dear?" she asked.

Maddie, whose little chin had been quivering, shook her head with her eyes closed and pressed Woofies against her face. Anna moved hair from her daughter's face, but made sure to stay clear of the bruise and cut on her chin. It had happened when they were thrown into a van. Maddie had howled—until a man threatened to slit their throats if they didn't shut up. They both wept, but did so silently.

Her daughter had survived. That was the important thing.

Anna looked to the door, wondering if the man with the slight limp would return with a blanket as he'd promised, then went back to gently rubbing her daughter's head while humming one of her favorites, "Twinkle, Twinkle Little Star."

Truth be told, she hummed the tune as much to calm herself as her daughter.

The barren room was void of any furniture. Blank walls, a cold concrete floor. A single metal toilet at the far end.

Anna's back ached from sitting against the wall, but her heart ached even more. As she clinched her jaw, her eyes burned. From the lack of sleep. From the lack of humanity.

They threatened to kill your daughter. And you.

Anna took in a full breath and felt her back pop—how long had it been since she'd been able to breathe fully? Days. At least four, if she were to guess. And it was only a guess as night and day had seemingly merged into one long continuum.

But she would never forget the night her world was turned upside down.

Anna had just poured herself a glass of wine when four masked men broke into their home. Before she could run upstairs to protect her daughter, she was slammed to the floor, dragged through broken glass, the shards carving trenches in her face and neck. But she ignored the pain, only concerned with Maddie's well-being.

One of the men brought a kicking Maddie downstairs. Before she could embrace her daughter, they were blindfolded, threatened with knives, and thrown into a van.

Later, they were transferred onto a plane which traveled at least twelve hours—three Maddie naps—before landing. After emerging from the aircraft, Anna had taken in the pungent odor of rotten fish, a suffocating humidity in the air.

The man with the limp had been the only person to interact with Anna. The only one to provide food and drink, two meals per day. The only one to speak to her directly.

"Your husband is on a very important mission for us. Once that is completed, you and your daughter will be returned," he'd said when putting them in the room.

My Jack. Could he really save us?

Before a smile could part her lips, her thoughts were hijacked by a dawning realization that grew stronger by the second. As a high school AP history teacher, Anna had a deep understanding of other societies, including their views toward women. She'd read countless stories where, in some countries across the world, women and girls were treated as pieces of property, sold to the highest bidder in seedy black markets. By her best estimate, she believed they were being held somewhere in the Far East. Where women and girls were being trafficked with alarmingly high frequency.

Anna's mind had searched for hope, but her inside voice wouldn't shut up until she acknowledged a very possible but harsh reality: neither she nor Maddie would see Jack again. The people who ran this operation would never allow them to be free. She and Maddie would be sold into slavery.

Maddie released a painful whine, her night tremors, and Anna realized she'd stopped humming. As she resumed the tune, a resolve consumed her. She would do everything in her power to keep her daughter safe.

Even if she had to sacrifice her own life.

7

Macau, China

The old man snorted out a restless grunt, the leathery flesh between his eyes snapping into a rigid crease. My head twitched at the sound and movement. I'd mistakenly thought the white-haired man was in a deep, slumbering sleep—or worse. He sat awkwardly in a rickety metal chair that tilted to one side in the sand. His skeletal appendages draped across rusted metal and shredding plastic, as if he'd collapsed in the chair. Perhaps he was sleeping off a drunken binge.

Lights shimmered across the dark water of Lago Nam Van. The unmistakable golden glow of Casino Lisboa in the heart of Macau's Central District. The irony of the old man's seemingly simple existence in the shadow of such opulence resonated with me.

A gentle breeze blew in from the sea, and I took in a salty breath.

Another glance at the old man's setup. He'd constructed a net-and-wire display of fresh fish. Like many of the merchants in Macau, all products were available for just a few patacas. The research from Simon gave me at least some confidence I could survive in this foreign land.

I resumed my moderate walking pace along the narrow stretch of rock-embedded concrete hemming the beach. Nearly the entire eleven-square-mile peninsula was drenched in colorful lights. The Las Vegas of the East could probably be spotted from the International Space Station two hundred miles above the planet, but I was on the one stretch that ended in a cone of darkness.

My dress shoes crunched along the sandy walkway. It was the only significant sound outside of an occasional wave and the faint buzz from the partiers on the balconies of Lago Nam Van—a name symbolic of the cultural merger of Portugal and China.

Beads of sweat bubbled at my hairline. Not surprising given the high humidity that was typical in this region of the world. I curled a finger inside the collar of my starched shirt, a bow tie clutching my neck. The tuxedo was an Armani, notched lapel and made of virgin wool. Expensive, yes, but essential to the execution of my mission.

I swung my sights to the right, away from the water. The faint lights of the city that never slept. Hong Kong, about forty miles east of Macau across the South China Sea. I'd visited Hong Kong as a teen. A few good memories with a father who'd pawned me off to my grandmother to be raised. My mother had died from cancer when I was a toddler. Back then, before the mass investment that turned Macau into a gambling mecca, the sleepy city was still under the control of the Portuguese, but its commerce was mostly ruled by the local Triads.

I strolled and scanned. Not a soul in sight. I could feel the bulk of the pistol stashed in a shoulder holster under my tuxedo jacket. I'd just purchased the sidearm in the last hour when word reached me about this meeting. A Sig Sauer P226. I wished I found the weapon comforting. But nothing about this undertaking was even remotely normal.

For the twelve hours since arriving in Macau, I'd maintained the public persona I was given. My credentials bore the name of Clayton Fishbeck, England-born, with degrees from Georgetown in DC and Oxford University in the UK. Fishbeck was a savvy businessman with an entrepreneurial spirit. He'd founded five technology companies, two of which had been sold for high seven-figure prices. But the other three had lost almost as much. He'd also made a short-term investment in a mixed martial arts organization, a rival to UFC. Fishbeck was a guy who had won big and lost big. He was looking for the right kind of opportunities to diversify his portfolio.

How Simon had created my new identity was a mystery. They obviously had access to certain systems, or the people who ran those systems. This network of Simonites had to be enormous, though it was entirely possibly it was just one person pulling all the levers.

Up to this point, I'd nearly drowned myself in questions I simply couldn't answer about Simon. I'd hoped to figure out a vulnerability with this group and expose it so I could rescue Anna and Maddie and move on with our lives. But no shortcut existed. None that I'd seen thus far. I had only one path forward: to carry out this mission as swiftly as possible.

According to the data I'd read as I flew across the ocean, this entire operation was drenched with blood money—a hideous process to traffic young women to the 2.2 billion people within a five-hour flight from Macau. While evidence of direct involvement by any one individual had been difficult to verify, the cyber-money trail appeared to intersect with the Waterfall Casino. It had recently undergone a change in management. A business coup, as it turned out. And the one leading the rebellion was a British ex-pat, Arthur Robinson.

My best hope—right now, my *only* hope—to learn about a possible connection between Robinson and the trafficking operation stood somewhere in the darkness in front of me. Simon had arranged for me to meet a former member of a prominent Triad called Y2K. I walked to within fifty yards of the agreed-upon meeting place, where trees hovered over the narrow walkway. Slowing my pace, I stepped more deliberately to reduce my noise footprint, squinting to pick up the outline of any figure.

The packed envelope nudged my ribcage. It held cash. Fifty thousand Hong Kong dollars. That was the price the kid had demanded to share his inside knowledge of the trafficking operation. To make matters even stickier, there was a real possibility of a major public relations nightmare if the Chinese were to learn that Robinson, a Brit, was at the helm of such an insidious business venture. PR was not high on my priority list, not unless it impacted my ability for this mission to succeed.

To save my dear Anna and Maddie, I would carry out these perilous orders, even if I had to step in the middle of an international hornet's nest.

"Stop where you go," a voice called out from somewhere in the thicket of dense vegetation. His English was solid, a trait shared by many in Macau.

I complied, and when I stopped, my elbow bumped my pistol. My instinct told me to grab it, but I tamped down the urge. Reaching for it was not a good play. The voice sounded fairly young with a slight lisp. He had to be the informant, a member of one of the most vicious Triads in Southeast Asia.

"I've come alone, as you requested. And I brought your money. Please show yourself so we can speak face to face." I quietly spun my body in a full circle. In the darkness, all I could make out were low-hanging branches and a single shaft of light shooting through the tree canopy ten feet in front of me.

"Put the money on the ground," the young man said.

"We need to talk first." My tone purposeful, but not overbearing.

Leaves rustled just above my head. I jumped back two steps as my hand clutched the grip of the gun. But I didn't remove it from the holster.

A figure dropped from a branch, landing in an athletic stance six feet away.

"Ubaldo?"

"It is me. Nothing to worry about."

8

I made sure Ubaldo could see my hands—*no weapons here*—and said, “You know how to make a dramatic entrance.”

The kid wiped his brow, then swiveled his head in either direction. He was no taller than I had been at age fourteen, about five-five. He was cut, with hard curves of muscles in his chest and shoulders. During his time with Y2K, he surely needed every fiber of his strength to survive amongst the sharks.

“I am here. That is what I promised,” he said.

“Do you mind if I shine my phone light so we can see each other better?”

The kid stuck out a defensive arm. “Let me,” he said, then pulled out his phone.

Seconds later, I was blinded, and I jerked my head to the side to block the targeted beam of light. “I can’t see a thing. Can you change the angle?”

“Sorry. Is that better?”

Streams of shadows and light streaked across his face. He

had Asian features and a gold-hoop nose ring. While I'd never visited Macau during my brief visit to Hong Kong as a youngster, I'd learned about the kids with Portuguese names and Chinese genes. The Macanese.

"Thank you."

Ubaldo's dark eyes tracked my hand, which I'd just put into my front pocket. I slowly removed my empty hand.

"The money. You have it on you?" he asked.

I tapped my coat pocket. "Tell me what you know about this trafficking operation. The girls."

Ubaldo let loose a sigh and blinked once, both movements long and slow. "I only know about the drugs. It's bad shit. Purest form of heroin we have seen since…I don't know when."

He ran his fingers through his hair, and I caught a glimpse of a headband. Red, black, and white. There was an image of some kind, but I didn't get much of a look before his raven-black hair dropped, covering it back up.

"Drugs are bad. We've known that for centuries. I need details—how the drugs are smuggled into China, how the money is laundered, the distribution process, and most importantly, names. I need names if there's any hope of putting a stop to this insanity." I figured the drugs and human trafficking were most likely part of the same operation. If I had to take a slightly different path to reach my goal, then so be it.

Ubaldo pursed his lips and bowed his chest. "You…you do not know what it means to be addicted," he spat out. "Your people brought drugs to my country, treated us like trash. Took our money and got us hooked for life."

A reference to the Opium Wars of the nineteenth century.

Muscles rippled in the kid's forearm as he balled his hand into a tight fist. The kid was strong, formidable even. While I had a few skills from my time as a college decathlete, I was no trained assassin. Did Ubaldo see me as friend or foe? Right now,

I was leaning toward foe, which is why I shifted my weight toward my toes, ready to react in a split second. I hoped it wouldn't come to that. For his sake and mine.

"We can't rewrite history, Ubaldo. I want to stop the drugs, end the senseless killing. Are you with me?" I attempted to align our interests—his drug concerns and my focus on the human trafficking. I wondered about the catalyst for the kid's rage. Was it purely historical in nature, or could there be a more contemporary influence stirring his emotions?

The kid held his gaze, narrowing his eyes as if considering his options. I noticed a drop of sweat bubbling at the edge of his brow. Then a slight twitch. Shadows flickered across Ubaldo's face. His hand holding the phone was trembling.

A pellet of unease pinged my gut. I took one step backward, focused on Ubaldo's simmering expression. I resisted the urge to draw the Sig, hoping like hell I could avoid a bloody scene. But something was off. I pushed out a slow breath and channeled my focus. The mission couldn't be compromised, even for a kid who'd broken free of the crime-ridden shackles of the Y2K Triad.

In that deciding moment, the kid's lips parted, and the ball of fury and hate etched on his face softened. His eyes wandered, scanning the ground, then back up at me.

"Ubaldo, we can work this out. I have the money, and you want a new life. Just tell me everything you know."

"I-I want to…" he said, his mouth agape.

I leaned forward, waiting to hear the affirming words. Leaves jostled overhead. Footsteps nearby. I did a fast one-eighty, lowering myself into a crouch and reaching for my gun at the same time.

Another kid was mid-swing with nunchucks. My fingertips were on the grip of my weapon, but I abandoned the attempt and thrust my arm upward. The muscled meat of my shoulder absorbed the impact as I kicked his legs out from beneath him. Connected with the side of his knee. Bones crunching, ligaments ripping. He cried out as the nunchucks fell from his hand, clanging to the sidewalk.

I threw the gangbanger to the ground and hit him with a straight right cross. The punch connected to the attacker's larynx, and he flailed uncontrollably.

A sharp prick in my shoulder. In the millisecond it took me to swing my head around, a tar-like substance coated my mind. My limbs became jelly. I teetered, my equilibrium completely distorted. There was shouting, and I blinked rapidly, but my vision became blurry. Figures jumped up and down, pointing at me as my body bounced off the unforgiving concrete.

How many were there?

Bony knees slammed into my back, but somehow I kept hold of the pistol. Using both hands, as shaky as they were, I raised the Sig, aiming it in the general direction of the blurred motion. Pulled the trigger.

A wailing shrill pierced the air. The bullet had hit a target. The person on my back lunged over my head and clawed at the gun. Wrenching my body as much as I could, I felt him sliding off me. I steadied the gun, took in a breath, and…

A leather boot swung across my vision, slamming into my hands. The gun discharged, flew off to the side. I pushed my body upward, but knees jabbed into my kidneys. I collapsed back to the ground. Eyes open, another boot kick. No way to stop it. The blow rattled my brain. I quickly became a punching bag for brass-knuckled fists and whirling nunchucks.

One more breath, and darkness swallowed me whole.

9

I was one foot out the door when my grandmother called for me. I debated pretending not to hear, but I knew there would be severe consequences once she caught up to me. I marched back into the living room, where she paused her latest crocheting project to hand me an envelope.

"Mrs. Everton finally paid for the shawl that I made for her daughter. Get to the bank before it closes."

"Mama, I finally have a day off from track practice, so I was going to meet some friends and…"

Her eyebrows had started the slow climb up her forehead. It was pointless to push back. I got into her twenty-year-old pickup and drove to the bank downtown, slipping in the front door at five minutes before closing time. The teller handled the three people in front of me in quick order, and as I stepped forward, I hoped that I'd still be able to catch up with my friends in the Sonic parking lot.

"Here you go," I said, sliding the cash envelope across the

counter.

The teller didn't move. She didn't blink. Her jaw fell open, and she stumbled backwards.

A man wearing a ski mask pushed me to the side and aimed a gun at the young lady. "Empty your drawer. Here." He threw his backpack at her, but she didn't move, and it dropped to the floor.

"Did you hear me?"

As my pulse took off in a sprint, I looked around for the on-duty cop. No sign of him. Everyone else was ducking for cover.

The woman started to shake uncontrollably.

"If you don't comply to my demands, I'm gonna..." He waved the gun at her over the counter, and she screamed. But she still didn't act.

"Dammit, woman!" He turned quickly, and his menacing gaze landed on me. Grabbing my arm, he yanked me into his chest and put the gun to my head.

"You fill that bag with cash, or I put a bullet in this kid's head. Got me?"

Her eyes met mine, and for a moment, I wondered if she was frozen with fear. After a painful count of two, she picked up the backpack and stuffed cash into it, and the man snatched it from her hand.

"Now that's how to do it," he said with a wheezy chuckle.

Just as I started to pull away, the cop emerged from an office, his gun at the ready.

"Go ahead and shoot," the robber said, backing us toward the exit. "My teenager pal here would love to eat some lead. Right?" He looked at me.

"No," I said.

He snickered some more, then banged the door open with his foot without making a misstep. Outside, he started to run, but he never let go of my arm.

"Hey, you got your cash, so let me go."

"No fucking way. You're my ticket out of this shit town." He shoved me into the driver's seat of a sedan and told me to drive.

Five miles later, we were on a country road and the man was singing, smoking a joint, and counting his cash. I knew my life was about to end. He'd either put a bullet in my head or force me to be his accomplice, which would surely end in death.

"Stop."

"Huh?" I said.

"You heard me. Stop the car."

I felt the blood drain from my face. This was it—I'd be shot and left to the vultures. When I slid the gear into Park, *he swung the butt of his pistol into my head three, four, five times, then kicked me out of the car.*

He drove away. Against all odds, I'd lived. And I was damn thankful.

Two hours later, drained and nursing countless bruises, my track coach showed up at Mama's house.

"Thanks for coming over," I said, pulling a bag of frozen peas off my lip.

The man who cussed me out on a regular basis gripped my shoulder and looked me in the eye. "Jack, when I first heard about the bank robbery, you want to know my first reaction? I thought it was you who'd robbed the bank."

"No shit?"

He nodded. "Unless you stop running with the wrong crowd, you're going to end up dead in a ditch. Do you understand what I'm saying, boy?"

I nodded, but in reality, I was still processing what he'd just said.

He started to walk off but turned back and, again, put his hand on my shoulder. "Your talent is off the charts, Jack. More than that, though, you are the most fiercely determined athlete I have ever seen. You want to know what me and the other coaches call you? The Barracuda. Mentally and physically tough. Unbreakable. You just have to believe in yourself."

***

Unknown location

I awoke when a kid hurled a cup of water at my face. The cup bounced off my nose, and I lapped up every drop of water my tongue could reach.

"You!" he barked.

It was one of the gangbangers who'd ambushed me. I blinked a few times and realized my weight was being supported by ropes around my wrist. I glanced down. More rope around each ankle. I felt bruises all over my face and neck, up and down my back. I was damn lucky they hadn't killed me. But what was their endgame?

He stepped closer, setting his jaw. I ignored the water clinging to my chin and stared at him, now only six inches from his face.

"You killed my brother. My only brother."

Air rushed from my lungs. The punch to that one kid's larynx. I'd never killed another person. Never had any weird fascination to do so. The jab I'd thrown was just a reflex. But it had killed him.

"I…" Words wouldn't come out.

The kid slipped a set of brass knuckles onto his good hand and cocked his fist. "In our world, there is only one way to resolve this."

I wasn't sure any words would stop what was about to happen, and I couldn't break free to give myself a fighting chance. I'd have to take the punishment. It couldn't be worse than the mental torture I'd been experiencing over the last five days.

I lowered my head slightly and constricted my muscles, priming for the first blow.

Someone screamed.

10

Our eyes jerked toward the door. "Wen!" the woman repeated.

She crossed the threshold, her long leather boots clipping the hardwoods. She wore tight black jeans. A gray, ribbed tank top clung to her figure, her black hair in a severe ponytail. Despite the scowl folding her brow, she was striking.

She carried a brown stick, thin and flexible. She tapped the stick into her opposite hand as she approached the kid.

"This is not the right time, Wen."

He pulled back his fist. "He killed my brother!"

She grabbed his hand and didn't let go. The muscles in her upper arm rippled. "I said, not now."

"Wen, chill out, man." Ubaldo rambled through the door. "I hate it that your brother died, but doing this won't bring him back."

Wen huffed out a breath and relaxed his fist. Ubaldo popped Wen's shoulder and guided his friend over to the corner, throwing a passing glance in my direction. Surprisingly, I didn't sense any festering hatred from Ubaldo. It puzzled me, as did the purpose behind them keeping me alive this long. Perhaps they thought I had information that would benefit them even more than the cash they'd stolen from me.

"Eyes on me." The woman smacked her stick against the side of her leg.

"That won't be difficult." I snapped back in character as my mind flashed through images of my beautiful wife. *Anna, I'm doing this for you and our daughter—you know that, right?*

She sauntered forward a few steps and brushed the end of the stick against my cheek. I flinched as it grazed one of my many wounds. The stick was made of soft leather. I took another gander at her outfit and the muscled compactness of her body.

"You're a jockey?" I asked.

The crease of her lips turned upward. "Maybe I am. Maybe I am not. But I want to know who you are."

"My ID is in my back pocket. Have a look."

"Do you think we are stupid, Mr. Clayton Fishbeck?"

"So there, you already know my name. Can you cut these ropes now?"

The conversation happening in the corner of the room became louder.

"I don't care what you say to me." Wen thumped his chest. "I cannot forget my brother." He turned on his heel and walked toward the door. Midstride, he jabbed a finger at me. "No matter what happens with…all of this," he said, swirling his arm in a circle, "it's you and me in the end, dude. And there won't be anyone around to save your sorry ass."

He stormed out of the room, Ubaldo right behind him. The door slammed shut.

Despite the threat, a confrontation with Wen was low on my worry list. My main concern was getting blood flow into my arms. Then gaining my freedom so I could fulfill my mission—

get Anna and Maddie back.

The jockey went to the door, opened it a crack, craned her neck, and looked outside. A smattering of distant light. We had to be in a populated area, possibly still Macau. She flipped around and strode back to me, then paused, her eyes boring into mine. The whirring engine of a vehicle buzzed just outside the door, but the noise didn't alter her focus.

She leaned closer, her voice subdued. "I need to know who you really are. It is important."

I detected a vulnerable, almost desperate edge in her tone. I studied the woman. She was fit, with a fiery spirit. As the yellow bulb's glow illuminated her deep-set, brown eyes, there was a soft layer beneath her powerful exterior.

"What exactly is so important to you?" I asked.

"I think you know, which is why you met Ubaldo. To learn more information."

I wasn't in a position to play coy, but revealing my true identity wasn't in the cards. "I'm in the IT business. I founded five different startups. Perhaps you've heard of them?"

She swatted an irritated hand just in front of my face, causing me to flinch. "We have your pistol. What kind of businessman carries a Sig Sauer P226 in a shoulder holster?"

"I knew I was meeting with someone dangerous. Basic protection."

"A so-called IT entrepreneur seeking information about a human trafficking operation? That is absurd."

"We all have our causes," I said.

"You will not play these games with me!"

I stared at her.

She tapped her whip into the palm of her opposite hand. "Shortly, I will know. I have sent your picture off to Beijing."

"You're not a jockey, are you?"

She flipped around and walked to the chair, resting her hands on the back of the seat. Strumming her fingers along the vinyl. Eyeballing me.

"Who do you know in Beijing?" I asked.

Her gaze drifted away from me and off to a corner of the room. "You know."

I thought back to the material I'd reviewed and the warnings I'd received from Simon. "MSS?"

She paused for a second, then nodded. "But it is not what you think."

"Hmm. I'm being held captive, tied up in a dirty building by an agent of the Chinese Ministry of State Security. I'd say I have a pretty good idea of what's going on."

"Tell me your real name," she said with more force.

"What are you doing hanging out with two former Triad members?"

"I need your help, Mr. …"

"Fishbeck. Some of my friends call me Fish for short."

She smacked the back of the chair. "We do not have long. It will be better for you, for me, for this situation if we can talk now, before Ubaldo comes back."

"What's this about Ubaldo?"

"He is my cousin."

I maintained a neutral expression.

"He does not know my real job."

I wondered if this was all part of a ruse. "So, your cousin thinks you're a jockey who drugs and kidnaps British businessmen in her spare time?"

She took in a deep breath, brought a hand to her face. "He knows I care about him. Helping to free him from this gang life is my priority."

"More than following the orders of your assignment?"

Her eyes tracked something across the floor. Looking for her next line to further reel me in? Finally, she brought her eyes back to mine. The hard edge had disappeared.

"I need to know I can trust you."

The vulnerability had returned to her voice, but that only heightened my suspicions of a ploy. I searched her concerned expression for any sign of deceit. Her eyes did not waver, and the stress through her neck and shoulders was obvious. She appeared authentic and convincing.

"Trust me to do what?"

She grunted and pursed her lips. "Do you know what MSS agents are authorized to do with enemies of the state?"

"I'm only an IT guy—"

She flicked her wrist, and the whip smacked the vinyl with a resounding *whap*. "Stop it! Now. I do not want to hear more of your lies. I am taking a huge risk by sharing all of this with you."

Her voice had pitched higher, another hint of anxiety. Maybe she was acting on her own, not as an assignment from MSS.

"Cut me down, and then we can talk."

"How do I know I can trust you? How do I know you will not run away or try to kill me?"

"If you want me to trust you, it's a first step." I glanced upward at my swollen hands, a sickening blue. "I won't be any good to anyone with no hands."

She cut the ropes around my wrists and ankles.

Relief. I wiggled my fingers and toes, focusing on getting the blood to flow normally again as she took a phone call, speaking in Cantonese. I had no idea what the topic of conversation might be. A minute later, she ended her call.

"Let us go for a walk, Mr. Jack Whitfield."

11

We stood on a grassy hill, just behind a row of single-story industrial buildings. By the glow of her cell phone, I could see the MSS agent smiling as she swiped through family photos. She stopped to show me one. “I was fourteen years old, and Ubaldo and I were swimming in the bay off Tapai, the south island of Macau. As cousins, we always played games, seeing who could jump the farthest off the pier.”

There was a resemblance between the two cousins at a younger age. She had told the truth, at least about how they were related.

“Who are the two kids running in the background?”

“They are…*were* my other cousins, Jia and Sam.” She stared at the screen an extra moment and swallowed hard. “So full of energy and life. It all changed once they moved away. They tried to make it in the big city, but it devoured them. Actually, the heroin devoured them. They both died from drug overdoses.”

“I’m sorry.”

"Now you can maybe see why Ubaldo and I are passionate to stop this new wave of drug trafficking."

I nodded. "I don't even know your name."

"Su Lien. Ubaldo and I are related through my mother's side of the family."

We shook hands. Her grip was firm, indicating a self-assuredness. Su had done nothing to make me think she wasn't being transparent. But my sixth sense couldn't help but wonder if we might be under surveillance. MSS agents could easily be hiding in a nearby building, taking pictures, using listening devices. She may not even be aware that a surveillance operation was happening.

I inhaled a deep breath and shook my hands at my side. The tips of my fingers were still tingling.

"I apologize for the extreme conditions in which you were brought to us."

"This whole setup was flawed. A kid was killed," I snapped.

"It was never my intent. They had instructions to only get close enough to jab the needle in your arm. These kids are trained to be violent, to go for the kill even when it is not necessary. But I should have known that. It is ultimately my fault. I will work through this with Wen."

I sensed her remorse but weighing that against her role as an MSS agent didn't sit well with me. It all seemed inconceivable, or at least perplexing.

"Won't be easy," I said.

"Oh, before we go further, this is yours. Or someone you work for." She placed the envelope of cash in my hand.

I stared at it for a second, then pushed it back to her. "Give it to Wen, his family. A life is worth far more than money, but maybe it will help a little as he starts his life outside the Triad."

"Ubaldo and Wen are still in."

"They're not *former* members?"

"That is their goal. Their leader, Liou Changming, is ruthless. They have already missed one of their security shifts down by the private dock. Liou will learn of their absence and possibly of their desire to leave Y2K. Maybe he has already. But Ubaldo could not keep quiet any longer, not with the death of his cousins haunting him."

"Are you working this mission solo? It's obviously very personal for you."

She paused a beat. "Officially, the MSS wants me to learn who is behind the drug trafficking operation and shut it down. But I do have skin in the game, yes."

I nodded. "Ubaldo knows who's running this operation?"

"He has suspicions of a group called Viper. Ubaldo has seen their symbol on the baggies of heroin. The same symbol is seared onto the young girls who are sold like fresh meat."

"They brand the girls?"

She took a hard swallow. "It is hideous."

Sickened by the thought, I turned away, rammed my fingers through my hair. My mind went straight to the last picture I'd received of Anna and Maddie. Anna's face showed stress but also strength. She had always been the rock of our family, and now she was the sole lifeline for our daughter. To stop their suffering, I had to find Cai Chen, and quickly.

"According to Ubaldo, Y2K was tasked with heading up local security once the drugs and girls reach port here in Macau. He believes the Viper organization is very large and complex."

I eyed the calm bay water in the distance. "Does Ubaldo have any other information to share? Any names or affiliations that might be useful?"

"He has tried to listen in on phone conversations, but only heard the name 'Waterfall Casino' mentioned a couple of times."

"What about it?"

"He is not very high up in Y2K, so his exposure to how

things actually work is minimal."

"Understood," I said, rotating my arm a few times, trying to work through some of the soreness in my shoulder.

"He did share with me one very gruesome scene." She paused as if waiting for my approval to proceed.

"How bad?"

"It was a grave, a mass grave of young girls. They were all beaten beyond recognition, discarded like trash. He believed they were killed on the cargo ship that brought them to Hong Kong."

"And then they are brought to Macau?"

A nod. "Speed ferries."

"We should be able to connect the boats to a person or corporation associated with Viper."

"Ubaldo said the boats have no markings or names. They were covered up to conceal their association with anyone."

"What about the docks they land at?"

"They change constantly, and only the leaders know where the speed ferries will land."

My cynical side still believed Su and the MSS could be enticing me to perform a certain heinous act so they wouldn't have blood on their hands, and then point the finger in my direction later. That would keep me from Anna and Maddie, and there was no way I would allow that to happen.

But my humane side couldn't ignore the other signs from Su. She had cut me loose, knowing I could try to harm her, or at least run. She'd shown me family photographs and, more than that, revealed a vulnerable part of herself. She cared for Ubaldo and clearly wanted him to find a new life away from the Triad. At the same time, she'd been given a mission by her superiors at the MSS—to uncover the person running the drug trafficking operation and shut it down. Our objectives in Macau appeared to overlap a great deal.

She reached out and gently touched my cheekbone. "You

have several abrasions. Ubaldo knows a cut man. We can get those fixed so the damage will appear like you nicked yourself shaving."

"I'm just an IT executive, here to do a little gambling, look for business opportunities."

She arched a shapely eyebrow. "I only know your name and that you live in Nashville, Tennessee. Our research has hit an unexpected roadblock. We will keep digging. I am almost certain, however, that your stories of being an IT executive are false. I suppose you have a bit of Louisiana swampland you want to sell me, no?"

"Eh." I shrugged.

"I know you must have your own loyalty to your government."

I said nothing, but it was clear she didn't know my connections or ultimate motivation. Not yet anyway. It was only a matter of time before the MSS information-gathering machine rooted out my complete story. Did the MSS have any knowledge of Simon? If so, getting access to that data could open the door for me to hunt down the bastards who stole my family. Many unknowns and questions. For now, the less personal information I shared the better.

"I can respect your position. I just need your help," she said.

"How?"

"You will be my date tonight."

12

Waterfall Casino
Cotai

Five rows back from ringside of a boxing match, I gazed at Arthur Robinson and his entourage. The new owner of the Waterfall Casino in Cotai had a gold cane, a walrus-like physique, and a loud personality—barking at people like an uncontrollable toddler. While the information on the big man was thick with data, very little was known about those in his inner circle. Publicly, he avoided sharing his organizational structure, only saying that he had close advisors who helped him manage his business and charitable affairs.

Su and I pulled out our phones and pretended to surf our respective social media accounts. In reality, we were sifting through the photos she'd received from her MSS handler to determine if there were any matches to those in Robinson's entourage.

"Food, drink before the fight begins, sir?" a large waiter asked.

I waved him off, then asked Su if she had any pain medication in her clutch. My entire body ached from the beating I'd taken.

As she searched her bag, I started to feel a distant urge clawing at my conscious thoughts. The one that would lead me to numbing all the pain, physical and otherwise.

She handed me two pills. "Ibuprofen? Anything stronger?" The bell clanged twice before she could answer, and people behind us started shouting at the same moment.

The boxing match featured two welterweights, both coming in at just under 147 pounds. The southpaw, a gentleman from the Philippines, reportedly had been Manny Pacquiao's sparring partner. He was the current Southeast Asian defending champion whose deft agility made him worthy of the title. He never stopped moving, and as the fight headed into the third round, his sneaky right-hand jab left his slow-footed opponent with a swollen eye and bloody nose. The opponent responded with wild right hooks that caught mostly air.

When the bell signaled the start of the eighth round, the challenger dragged his feet to center ring, while the champ danced around like some of the greats, Sugar Ray Leonard or even Muhammad Ali. He opened the round with two quick jabs and an uppercut, sending the challenger into the ropes. The crowd went wild.

"This is such a bore." Su rolled her eyes. "People can be so barbaric. I just do not understand the feeding frenzy."

"Coming from a lady who uses a whip on a horse," I said with a wry grin.

"It is a crop, not a whip. And who says I only use it on a horse?"

We turned our attention back to the Robinson crowd, most of

whom were on their feet, pumping their fists in support of one of the fighters.

During the fight, Su and I compared the MSS photos against Robinson's troop of bodyguards, bimbos, and advisors with their plus-ones. None of them were connected to illegal activity, according to our matches. The MSS apparently had tabs on everyone, even those with a seemingly insignificant existence.

One person remained unidentified. A man with dark, slicked-back hair in a black suit, silk shirt, and tie sat three rows behind Robinson but still inside the cordoned-off VIP section. He wore gold-rimmed sunglasses that were so large they covered his cheekbones. There was no way to get a detailed look at the man unless he removed his glasses. With his diminutive frame and oversized clothes, he would have appeared childlike had it not been for his widow's peak and a black, bristly patch of hair at the end of his pronounced jaw. He sat next to a man I assumed was a bodyguard—the guy's shoulders spanned two chairs. The mountain of a man had spiked, gelled hair.

The same waiter from earlier walked past our section. "Excuse me, sir," I said, lifting a hand.

He handed a beer to a customer then walked over, leaning in closely as the crowd cheered again. I gave him my drink order.

"Are you sure you don't want a double, sir?"

"Need to stay lucid this evening," I said, even though I craved anything but. "But I do have a favor to ask."

I palmed the waiter 4,000 patacas, and his chubby face stretched wide with delight. I explained what I needed him to do, and he nodded cheerfully, then walked away.

"Everything okay?" Su asked.

"It should be." The bell rang again, ending the ninth round. The challenger pawed at the shaking ropes and plopped onto a wooden stool in his corner. "We just need the fight to make it through the last round."

A couple of minutes later, my order arrived. “Cheers,” I said to Su before downing the shot with a single gulp.

“You’re not driving tonight,” she said.

“It was a single. Besides, we took a cab.” I crossed my legs, naturally pushing my line of vision to the right. “Keep a close view on the pencil-neck, flashy guy in the back over there.” I gestured with my chin.

As if on cue, the waiter walked up to the cord and called out to the bodyguard sitting on the opposite side of our mystery man. The waiter took a beer from his rack and reached across the man in the glasses to hand the beverage to the supersized bodyguard. But the extra-large cup slipped through the waiter’s hands—not accidentally—and beer gushed onto the mystery man.

He went berserk, jumping up, ripping off his glasses, and berating the waiter. Mock horror filled the waiter’s eyes as he tried to wipe the man’s suit and hair with napkins. The man jabbed a finger into the waiter’s chest.

At that exact moment, in the ring the defending champion unleashed a flurry of body shots, and his opponent dropped his gloves, releasing a guttural response. The crowd jumped to their feet and went nuts.

“Name is Shek Jian.” Su slipped her phone into her purse as we both stood. “He has ties to an Afghan drug lord.”

I gave her a quick double-take. “Did I miss that fact in the data?”

“It was not in the data you saw.”

Su had been holding out on me. She pushed past me.

“Hey, where are you going?” I asked.

She gestured with a nod at the Robinson group and marched toward the canopied exit. Shek Jian was leaving through an exit near him, the bodyguard on his heels. Was Su planning to confront them?

I questioned whether to follow her or stay put. She was, after all, a trained agent who could probably handle just about any situation. I also didn't want her to create a scene and blow our cover.

The decision was made for me. The champ knocked out his challenger, and after a brief round of whoops and hollers, the crowd began to disperse. I quickly regretted my hesitation. The throng of people leaving the arena clogged the pedestrian arteries. I methodically made my way through the crowd, resisting the urge to plow through everyone. Halfway up the ramp, someone tugged on my arm.

"Follow me." Su pulled me down a hallway where only a handful of people were walking.

I stumbled closer as her Jimmy Choos clipped the flooring with a staccato echo.

"What happened?" I asked, still trying to keep pace with her.

"I wanted to get close enough to attach a tracking device to him, but the bodyguard kept everyone ten feet away. Shek received a phone call and was headed for the exit. We have to follow him."

The chase was on.

13

The corridors of the Waterfall Hotel and Casino went from a trickle of people to a 100-year flood in about ten seconds.

"Do you still see him?" Su tugged on my suit coat, trying to pull herself taller.

Two drunk men stumbled into me. The one with a yellow jacket spilled his drink on my sleeve. Ignoring them, I pushed the canary out of the way. I got to my toes and spotted the spiked hair of Shek's bodyguard up ahead.

"Spike. I see him."

The moment I turned toward Su, she was swallowed up by a new rush of patrons. I whipped my head around. Spike turned left. I assumed Shek was with him. Back to Su—the wave of people had shoved her even farther away.

Leave Su and go after Shek myself, or grab her and maybe lose Shek in the process? I volleyed that decision for about two seconds. She knew the city; I didn't.

I backtracked, squeezing through people who acted like I

didn't exist. I was no hockey player, but I knew how to throw a hip check. And I did. Four of them. Without creating a riot.

"Take my hand," I said to Su once I reached her.

"I don't need you to rescue me."

"I did it for me."

"Did you let Shek get away?"

I looked at her, dumbfounded. "Me? What—"

A fist came out of nowhere and connected with my jaw. Flashing circles lingered in my vision. The space started to spin as I struggled to stay upright. I threw a punch at something moving, but I whiffed, lost my balance, and stumbled to the floor.

Voices all around me, feet stomping near my hands. I had no idea who had attacked me or why, but I rubbed my eyes, took in a fortifying breath, and pushed myself up to a standing position, ready for a fight.

The man in a yellow suit had just handed his coat to his buddy. Canary took one step in my direction and threw a roundhouse right. I ducked and hurled a punch into his ribs.

"You're gonna regret doing that," he growled into my ear. His hand reached inside his pocket. The grip of a small pistol became visible. I lunged at him, but he spun away. I quickly executed my own spin move and...

"Stop!" Su kicked out and jabbed her stiletto heel straight into Canary's wrist. He yelped, dropping the gun. A second later, Su had some type of death grip on the area just below his shoulder. The man released a high-pitched wail and rattled off something in Cantonese.

"You will leave us alone," she said.

"Anything, anything you say, lady. I can't feel my arm. The pain…ah!"

The crowd began to part. Security guards were marching toward us. I grabbed Su's free hand and led us in the opposite direction. “Gotta go.”

“That man deserved to lose his arm.”

No time to discuss the pros and cons of hand-to-hand combat. A glance over my shoulder. Two security guards were speaking with Canary and his buddy. Just as they pointed in our direction, I ducked lower to blend in with the crowd and cut left down the same corridor Spike had just gone down. Su was right on my heels.

“We lose them?” I asked.

We picked up the pace, and as we motored through the front lobby, I could see the small, wiry Shek walking outside.

“I don’t see either one of them,” she said when we reached the twenty-foot glass doors.

I panned the circular drive where people and cars zipped around. “Off to the right. They’re walking.”

“That means we’re following.” She looped her arm around mine, and off we went. Before Shek and Spike had made it to the edge of the building, they veered off to the left. “Are they…?” I arched my neck to look up at the light rail station hovering above the street.

“The LRT. Surprising that someone with access to a lot of money would take mass transportation,” Su said.

“Maybe he knows he’s being followed.”

“It could simply be part of his travel protocol.”

Once Shek and Spike made it up to the LRT landing area, Su and I blended in with a group of folks headed up the same staircase.

We purchased a day pass from one of the vending machines and casually waited for the next train while keeping an eye on Shek. I jumped when a hand brushed my back.

“It is only me,” Su said. “You are so jittery. Have you forgotten your training?”

“In terms of assessing a company’s true market value based

on their projected income and assets? Actually, yes, I studied at—"

"You are full of shit, Jack Whitfield. And it is only a matter of time before I know the full truth."

How that would impact my mission or our working relationship was difficult to predict. Ignoring Su's comment, I rested my elbow on the pillar behind her. "What is Shek doing now?"

"Checking his phone. Oh, he is now looking this way." She peered into my eyes and patted my cheek.

"Nice adjustment. You've been trained well."

She mumbled something. I started to turn my head, but she grabbed my face and planted a kiss on my lips.

14

On the LRT
Cotai

When Su finally let go, I wiped my mouth. "What the hell was that?"

"You now have a Southern twang to your voice, Clayton Fishbeck."

"Was it really necessary for you to—"

"Come on." She pulled me onto the train, and we found a pair of seats. Shek sat by himself at the back of the train, and Spike was two rows away. Between us and them was a throng of people gabbing away in multiple languages—plenty of cover for us to blend in and observe.

The instructions to be seated or hold on to a rail was projected through the speakers in Cantonese, Portuguese, and English. Three beeps followed. When the train pulled away, one young lady in a pink halter dress who hadn't anchored herself stumbled, and the drink she was carrying sloshed over the side, splashing onto Shek's shoes.

Su nudged my ribs. "It could derail Shek's plans," she said.

"I see it. Hope we don't have an incident," I said quietly.

Spike grabbed the girl's wrist, and it wasn't gentle. I started to rise out of my seat, but Su pulled me back down.

"I can't let him hurt her. It's not right."

"Hold on." Su gestured with her chin toward the front of the train.

Two men wearing fishnet shirts approached Spike and got in his face.

"This could get ugly," I said.

"Shek might just call it a night and go home. We could miss our one opportunity to see if he's connected to Viper."

"Dammit." I was pissed. At the girl for not paying attention to the instructions. At Spike for being so aggressive. I turned to Su, ready to repeat my irritation at her unsolicited kiss. "And by the way—"

"We just got lucky." She poked my ribs, and I returned my focus to the scene before us.

Spike threw some cash on the floor, and the two fishnet guys scooped it up and rejoined their friends.

"Crisis averted for now." I kept watching, though. Spike pulled some type of cloth from his pocket, lowered to one knee, and wiped off Shek's shoes while Shek continued gazing out the window.

The party crowd stole our attention, and I welcomed the distraction. The buzz reminded me of better times, hanging out with family and friends. Times filled with laughter and love. Now I was crushed beneath the weight of some evil force. A force I was now working for to save my wife and daughter. The dissonance of it all nearly stopped my heart.

Sadness quickly morphed into fury. To stop the quiver in my

chin, I stuck my fingernail into my wrist, which pulled my thoughts back to the moment.

Focus on the objective, one step at time. You can do this. You WILL do this.

Su put a hand on my thigh. “Are you okay?” Her eyes matched her compassionate tone. But I stared at her hand until she pulled it back.

“I don’t mean to be…”

Three beeps sounded, and the train began to slow again. Su arched her back and glanced out the window.

“What’s special about this stop?” I asked.

“It is near the back entrance of Studio City. The property is the size of a small city. Easy to lose people.”

As luck would have it, Shek and his bodyguard exited the train and headed down to street level. Amidst a large crowd, we hustled to the bottom in time to see the pair in front of an elaborate arched stone entrance that had *Studio City* written across the top, massive bronze pillars anchoring either side. The enormous hotel and casino building hulked on the far side, bathed in purple lights. Smaller establishments ringed the property.

In they went, and so did we.

15

Studio City
Cotai

After navigating a winding trek through the Studio City property, we entered the building and searched for Shek and Spike.

"There," Su said, already taking my hand and pulling me along. "They turned into the Premiere Bar."

"Meeting someone for late-night drinks. Could be worth our while," I said.

"*If* that person is involved in Viper."

"You have doubts," I said.

"Instincts matter. But proof matters more."

The crowd in the bar was lively but subdued. Someone was playing a snappy tune at a grand piano. A Billy Joel song. After sitting in the last two empty chairs, a white-gloved waiter handed us menus and said he'd be back to take our order. I set the menu on the table, my eyes on Shek and Spike at the small bar. They didn't sit right next to each other, instead allowing an empty barstool between them.

"Here. Order something." Su pushed the menu toward me.

"I'm not hungry or thirsty."

"To stay under the radar, Jack, we must order drinks like everyone else. I will keep an eye on Shek while you look at the menu."

Grudgingly, I did as she said. When the waiter dropped by, he first asked Su for her order.

"I'll have a London Love Story."

"If that's the case," I said, "I'll take a Kabuki."

"It is Japanese," she said after the waiter had left.

"Does that matter?"

She shrugged, and we both took a casual glance toward the bar. The chair next to Shek remained empty. Still wearing his gold-rimmed sunglasses, he sipped from a flute of champagne but spoke to no one.

"Not exactly Mr. Social," I said.

"He has a bad vibe."

The drinks arrived. We clinked our glasses and took sips, my eyes still shifting to Shek every few seconds. The wiry man just stared at his drink as if that was the only company he desired.

Just as Su leaned toward me to speak, a middle-aged couple walked in with a girl who appeared to be in her early teens—she looked just like her mother. Everyone at home said the same about Maddie and Anna.

My girls.

Su spoke, but I wasn't listening. Shek had just turned on his barstool, lowered his sunglasses, and ogled the teen as she walked past the bar. This dude was pure trash. He had to be connected to the human trafficking operation.

Su touched my arm. "I saw that," she said.

I tapped my foot off the floor like I was on speed.

"You are upset," Su said.

"I can't help it. He's involved in the trafficking—I know it in my bones. I want to rip his head off his torso, but only after I question him."

Shek now had a phone to his ear. After a couple of nods, he pocketed the phone, dropped some cash on the bar top, and scooted off his barstool.

"He's on the move," I said, practically leaping to my feet.

Su invaded my personal space, her hands gripping my waist.

"I, uh…"

"We must not overreact."

"Right."

She let go of me, and I inhaled a breath.

A count of three, then she said, "Now we can go." She turned and made a beeline for the exit. I flipped some bills onto the table and followed.

I somehow managed to not chase after her or the two men, ensuring I didn't create any unnecessary attention. I was a slow learner, but at least a few lessons had stuck. I finally caught up to Su at the casino's front doors.

"See them?"

"They are getting into a Mercedes. The black one."

I saw Spike's hair just before he bent down to squeeze into the front passenger's seat. "Shek is driving?"

"He is in the back. He has a driver."

"We need to follow them," I said, pushing open the door.

She gripped my wrist. The human handcuff.

"What now?"

She had her phone out and was speaking into it. "Wait just a few more seconds," she said to someone on the other end of the line.

"For…?" I asked.

She continued her phone conversation in Cantonese, firing off words like a machine gun.

“Su, we can’t let them get away. I can’t afford to play games.” I pushed through the door and searched for a taxi amongst the dozens of cars and people in the circular driveway.

“This way.” Su marched up to a blue limousine—actually, a Dodge Charger—that had just stopped.

“A blue limo?”

“Don’t have time to explain. Get in.”

After we’d slid into the back seat, Su instructed the driver in Cantonese, and he replied in kind.

“Don’t know what was just said, but I do hope he knows how to make this bugger go,” I said.

The driver tossed his hat to the side, turned around, and grinned, his white teeth glowing. “They call me Jet for a reason, Mr. Whitfield.”

16

Cotai

Jet turned the limo so quickly onto the main strip that Su almost fell into my lap.

"Jet! We must not draw unwanted attention. You should know that!" she shouted.

"But Mr. Whitfield said—"

"Jet!"

"Okay, okay." He slowed to a reasonable speed.

"And the name is Clayton Fishbeck," I grumbled, determined to maintain my façade. I searched for the black Mercedes and came up empty. "I'm not sure which way they went. We might have already lost them."

"I've been tracking them ever since I pulled up." Jet pointed straight ahead. "They took the roundabout and are still heading due south. They're just now passing the golf course."

"I think I see them," Su said. "Just behind that slower truck.

Jet, do your thing but keep your distance. Must not make a mistake."

"Yes, ma'am."

We passed a body of water on our left that looked more like a large moat. As we entered another roundabout, I spotted the black Mercedes on the far side. Jet, still behind a couple of cars, leaned into the curve, although I couldn't see his hands. I scooted up in my seat, and my eyes bugged out.

"No hands on the wheel?"

"Oh, sorry." With a nervous chuckle, he glanced at Su in the rearview. "An old habit of driving with my knee, back when I used to go joyriding in my father's taxi in San Francisco."

"Jet, you have interesting stories, but if you lose that black Mercedes, you can go back to San Francisco," Su said sternly.

His hands hit ten and two on the wheel. The amount of light outside the limo dropped back significantly, but the change in landscape was even more dramatic. No more tall buildings or loud advertisements. The road cut between two generous hills mostly covered by trees and brush.

"I can see your bewilderment, Jack," Su said. "This is Coloane. It used to be a lazy village. In some ways it still is, but probably not for long."

Once Jet turned the limo onto a narrow two-lane road, we traversed the base of the small mountain. Planes were arriving at the Macau Airport. Its main runway was a thin hem of land off the eastern coast.

The changing geography was nice enough, but I was chewing on why a kid from San Francisco was carrying out orders from an MSS agent.

My phone buzzed. I looked at my screen—a text from Simon. I gasped as I gazed at another picture of Anna and Maddie. They were both awake, each holding what looked like a piece of bread. Maddie was actually smiling, showing off her dimples. Anna had a hand on Maddie's back, anything to give our daughter comfort. Both had dark circles under their eyes, but it was good to see them eating. *If* it wasn't staged by their abductors to make me believe they were being treated humanely.

Just as I was about to pull my eyes away, I saw something on the wall behind Anna's shoulder. Smudged dirt. It was faint, but there seemed to be a pattern to the vertical and horizontal lines. It looked like Chinese writing.

Anna must have done it, and then positioned herself for the marking to be over her shoulder in the picture, hoping I'd see it. My wife knew a whole lot of things, but she didn't know squat about how to write in Chinese. This simply had to be a clue to let me know she was in China.

Did that mean they were in Macau, though? Ideas and theories cluttered my head, and it all quickly spun out of control.

A breath. I couldn't prove or disprove any of them.

Fuck.

A current of toxic electricity zipped through my veins, and all of my joints felt like they'd been plunged into a boiling grease pit. Watching my girls suffer, unable to rescue them, was beyond agonizing.

"Can I talk?" Jet asked.

"What?" I replied, quickly rolling down the window to allow air to hit my face.

"I might have an idea on where they're going,"

"Where?"

"Jack, he is just a kid. Not experienced in our line of work."

"I'm an IT entrepreneur."

She put her hand over her face. "Still playing the game."

"Guys, my idea is time sensitive," Jet said, waving one hand.

"Hands on the wheel!"

He quickly followed orders. "I need to say this. Please."

Clearly frustrated, Su let her arm drop to the seat. "What is it,

Jet?"

The limo slowed as Jet pulled to the side of the road. "Get out of the car."

"Why? What's going on?"

"They're turning into the small marina up ahead. You'll have a better chance of getting closer and scoping them out on foot. I'll find a place to stash the limo."

17

Coloane

Staying low to the ground, we walked through the rocky brush alongside the road, the terrain unforgiving. Especially for Su. She was in high-heeled shoes, but she moved easily and didn't complain. After pausing to allow a slew of cars to pass, we raced across the street and hunkered behind a rusting silver truck. I did a quick peek inside to ensure no one was sleeping.

"Clear?" she asked.

I nodded and peered around the side of the truck's cab. Down a slope, just beyond what looked like the marina office, people were milling about. But the view was limited because of the distance and lack of lighting. Su pulled up next to me.

"Does the Chinese culture understand personal space?"

"Does the Western culture understand necessary protocol to assess a potential target?"

I turned my sights back to the marina. Four dock workers

were loading supplies of some kind from a boat into a truck. I couldn't see much more than that, just moving figures with little detail.

"Can you tell if one of them is Shek?" I asked.

"Not sure."

"Damn dock workers just show up when we moved into position. It's like they're trying to mess with us."

"Jack, we need to be patient and give them a minute to finish their work."

"I don't have time to be patient. I've got—" I clamped my mouth shut to stop the flow of words and, even more importantly, to tamp down the rising tide of emotion.

Su chose not to respond to my outburst, keeping her eyes on the docks. I followed her gaze and studied the situation. The dock workers kept doing their thing.

"Even if those workers move on to do something else, I'm not sure we'll see what Shek and Spike are up to. The lighting is really poor," I said.

No response.

"We need another plan."

Still nothing from Su.

I nudged her. "Did you lose your hearing aid?"

She shot me an icy stare.

"Look, I have an idea that you're probably not going to agree with." I glanced back at the marina. Still only a blur of motion behind the dock workers.

"What are you talking about?"

I removed my suit coat and threw it into the bed of the truck. "You'll soon find out."

18

Full Moon Marina
Coloane

I ignored Su's biting calls from behind me. I had no choice. We weren't even certain that Shek was still in the marina. If he was, I wanted to know what exactly he was doing—and hopefully learn how it related to the trafficking operation. Alternatively, if Shek had worked us like a shell game, then I didn't want to waste any more time focusing on the marina.

As I walked toward the open gate to the marina, I rolled up my sleeves, undid the top button on my shirt, and messed up my hair. I walked toward the four dock workers, who were loading large bins of seafood into a refrigerated truck, sweating, grunting. Didn't even glance in my direction.

I circled the truck and zeroed in on the action at the far end of the pier.

"Can I help you?"

I startled and turned, cursing myself for not effectively using my peripheral vision. I had to get better at this game if I wanted to stay alive. A frumpy man in shades of gray stepped in front of me. Cap, T-shirt, hair, mustache—all gray. The clothes had some splashes of white paint on them.

"You sure can. I'm looking to rent a nice-sized boat."

"At this time of night?"

"Of course not. I just met this lovely lady—wow, what a knockout she is—and she has an affinity for boats."

"So, you want her to think you are a real man of the sea, just so you can get lucky?"

I smiled. "Not quite that simple. Plus, I'm more interested in the potential business prospects. She has some important friends who might come along."

He shrugged. "Everyone wants to be a Ho."

My eyebrows shot upward. "Excuse me?"

"Stanley Ho. Resident billionaire. Owns just about everything." He cocked his head and narrowed his eyes. "You want me to introduce you to him?"

"You know him?"

"I ran into him twice. He actually parked his boat right here at this marina once. Tipped me a thousand patacas. Saw him again at the club two months later, and he acted like he remembered me."

"Nice." I shifted my position so I could see down the dock again, but he moved in sync with me, blocking my line of sight.

"Come to my office, and I will see what boats we have available." He motioned toward the small building near the gate.

I knew I had to play this one out or he'd be suspicious. "After you," I said with one last look down the dock.

He walked with a slight limp but at a decent clip. He opened the door—it was the type that had a top and bottom half—and stepped inside. Closed the bottom half of the door, leaving me outside. He retrieved his laptop, set it on the bottom door ledge, and put on his readers. "Okay, when did you say you needed it?"

"I didn't. But how about tomorrow afternoon?" As he pecked away on the keyboard using his pointer finger, I leaned against the warped siding of the one-story building. Within seconds, I spotted Shek. His black silk shirt practically sparkled under the cone of a dim light. He was flanked by two men: an Anglo with slick-backed hair and an Asian man. Spike stood off to the side, surveying the area. When he looked in my direction, I turned back toward the gray man. Given my slight attire change—minus the coat, sleeves rolled up—I was hoping Spike wouldn't recognize me.

"What did you say your name was?" he asked.

"I didn't."

He paused his typing and looked at me.

"Clayton Fishbeck."

"You would butcher my Macanese name," he said, typing again. "Most Brits call me Tom."

Tom's mustache squirmed, and he went back to studying his laptop. I went back to observing the dock. More talking, not much action. While my first goal had been achieved—confirming Shek was at the marina—learning more about what he was involved in wouldn't be nearly as easy.

I recalled Su's brief comment about Shek back at the boxing match: *"He has ties to an Afghan drug lord."* There was no way to know if the two men talking to Shek might have similar ties, but I felt certain this midnight meeting wasn't to discuss gardening tips.

"Hey, Tom, you said Stanley Ho parked his boat here once. Do you get many high rollers?"

"Some who are. Some who just think they are," he said without taking his eyes off the screen. "Okay, how many folks did you say the boat needed to accommodate?"

"I didn't. Let's go with six."

"Okay, we have the… Wait, that will not work. Needs a repair. Well, we have the… Hold on, someone did not update the database." He tapped a few more keys and huffed out a breath.

I pulled out my phone to get a picture of the men with Shek. Maybe Simon could figure out who they were. Or I could have Su ask her MSS contacts to take a look. Regardless, I knew I couldn't act like a member of the Asian paparazzi. I put the phone back in my pocket.

"Okay, there are a couple of boats available. You really want to impress, right?"

I pulled my eyes away from Shek and gang. "Yep, it definitely needs to make an impression."

He tapped a finger on the screen. "This is the one. A repo, actually, but I think you will love it very much. The *Serendipity* is a splendid vessel. Sixteen meters, great power and efficiency in its Volvo IPS drive unit, three cabins, panoramic view from the living space. The Bavaria R55 is a spectacular boat."

"Sounds like you're their top salesman."

He grinned. "That would be my brother. He runs sales in Asia Pacific for them. That is how I got this repo. Ancient Chinese secret—it is not what you know, but who you know."

I doubted his take on the origin of that phrase. "Can I see it?"

"It needs to be cleaned up before you take it out tomorrow, but sure." He grabbed a set of keys, and we headed down the dock in the direction of Shek and associates.

Just as I'd hoped.

Fortunately, there was at least some activity between us and Shek, who was standing next to a large speedboat with his cohorts. Nearby, a man and woman were tethering their sailboat to a dock cleat while two young guys wearing Full Moon Marina shirts picked up trash.

"A fair amount of activity for this time of night," I said.

"Nothing compared to the marinas in Cotai and Taipa. The main peninsula is crazy busy all the time. We are a little more discreet here. And I do not ask a lot of questions."

A hand gripped my shoulder. I spun around while taking hold of the person's wrist, prepared to twist the assailant's arm until it snapped.

"Mr. Fishbeck, it's me, your driver."

19

Jet's audacity—actually, his stupidity—left me temporarily speechless.

"Jet, what are you doing here?" I could already feel Tom's stare but was more concerned that Shek and his people were also taking notice.

"I just want to help, you know."

I couldn't discount the idea that Jet might be purposely sabotaging this mission. Or was he just plain naïve? "Jet, can you please—"

"If you have a driver, then I guess you really do have the big money," Tom said, stroking his mustache.

Ignoring Tom's comment, I addressed Jet in a stern but subdued manner. "Okay, you can check out the boat we're going to rent for tomorrow's excursion."

Jet tilted his head, looking confused. Then his eyes shot open, and he nodded. "Roger that, Mr. Fishbeck."

Tom started walking along the dock as Jet pulled up next to

me. “Didn’t mean to scare you.” He offered a nervous chuckle.

I contemplated how I could use Jet to aid our cause. “Once Tom and I are on the boat, position yourself near Shek and his men, busying yourself with something, and try to listen in.”

“That’s why I’m here. If they speak Cantonese, I can interpret.”

Music played from one sailboat as a man on board gathered up the sails into a stowed position.

“Furling,” Jet said into my ear.

“What are you talking about now?”

“You’re watching that dude folding up his sails. It’s called furling.”

Jet’s mind never stopped. I wasn’t sure the net effect was a positive one.

Shek and his two associates didn’t acknowledge our presence as we walked past them. But Spike’s eyes locked on us. Did he recognize me from the LRT? I was positioned on the other side of Jet, but he was a few inches shorter than my six-one frame. Out of the corner of my eye, Spike turned his body in our direction. My breaths became shallower, but I maintained a casual posture. Would he pounce on us, try to question me? Warn Shek?

“Here it is, the *Serendipity*.” Tom stepped onto the finger of the dock next to the boat, and I followed behind him. When I glanced to my right, Spike was talking to Shek.

Dammit.

Jet bumped into my back. “Sorry, Mr. Fishbeck. I’m just dying to take a look at this boat. It’s absolutely sick!”

I rested a hand on his shoulder. “You can join our excursion tomorrow. For now, you’ll need to stay on the dock.” I gave him a wink before turning away. Now it was time for Jet to take the ball and run with it—listening in on Shek’s conversation. As long as Spike wasn’t in the process of alerting Shek about me.

That could ruin everything.

Once on board, Tom rattled off umpteen details about how the *Serendipity* was the perfect vessel, a combination of luxury and sporty. He took me on a tour, and I didn't protest. My eyes volleyed between Jet and the Shek meeting.

Jet inserted earbuds into his ear, held up his phone, and started to sway to the beat of music. I was stunned. He'd already forgotten his assignment.

I choked and released a loud cough. That actually made Tom pause his sales pitch. "You are not going to die on me, are you?"

I cleared my throat a few times. "All good. You were saying?"

"Right, the size of the tanks. Has two fuel tanks, both two hundred sixty-four gallons. And a good-sized water tank of one hundred fifty-eight gallons. Almost forgot to show you the main cabin. Just down these steps."

Inside the boat, I looked through the narrow windows. Jet was meandering along the dock just in front of Spike, who seemed annoyed by Jet's presence. While two dock workers dragged a number of heavy ropes down the pier, Jet dropped down to his knees, as if he'd fallen. I couldn't see what he was doing on the other side of the dock workers.

The workers moved on, and Jet swayed back in my direction.

Tom nudged my arm. "You know, for when you really need to close the deal with that hot lady friend." He smiled under his mustache.

I returned the smile, even though I hadn't heard his previous point. "Let's take one more quick tour of the deck area."

Up we went, and Tom paused at the stern to show me a built-in grill.

I said, "If you don't mind, I'd like to take some pictures of all this, just to get my lady friend extra excited."

He shrugged. As Tom kept himself busy cleaning up, I took

pictures. First of the boat. And when Shek and his two associates turned in my direction, I fired off about twenty shots. Turned out I didn't need Jet to create a diversion after all.

I finished the task and told Tom I'd be in touch. He handed me a business card, and Jet and I headed for the exit.

"You never gave me the signal," Jet said.

I told him how I'd been able to snap the pictures undetected.

"Very smart, Mr. Fishbeck…I mean, Mr. Whitfield."

I nodded and looked toward the rusty silver truck. No sign of Su. "Do you know where your boss is?"

A whistle. I followed the sound with my eyes. Su was down the road, waving her arms. Jet and I hustled in her direction, but she ducked behind a wall just before we got there. When we pulled around to the other side, she was shining her phone light for us. "Down here."

We hustled to the side of an abandoned building that was bordered by dense brush in the back. She was standing next to the Dodge limo, the rear door open.

"Good hiding place for the limo," I said.

"It was Jet's idea. But like you, he just walked off. He does not listen to orders."

Jet started cowering. I didn't. "He might work for you, but I don't. This is a partnership, not a dictatorship. No offense."

She released a noise that sounded like a growl.

"As you can see, I'm in one piece. So is Jet."

"Were you compromised?"

"For starters, we confirmed Shek was in the marina, meeting with two other men."

"Anything else? Did you figure out what he was doing there?"

"Not to the level I wanted. I did get a few pictures of the two men who were meeting with Shek. I was checking out a boat with the marina manager or whatever he was. Guy named Tom.

It was the perfect cover." I pulled my phone out and showed her the pictures.

"I will send those images to my handler at MSS. I am sure we can turn them around faster than MI6 or the CIA, or whoever your employer is."

Comparing the intel received from MSS and Simon might be helpful, even if I didn't know exactly how. Also, it wouldn't hurt to let Simon see the progress I was making. Anything to avoid them hurting my precious wife and child.

Su took the phone from my hands, placed the phones together, and the pictures were transferred. She typed a message to her contact, and I did the same with mine. There was a difference, though. She probably knew the person on the receiving end. For me, it was like communicating with a black box.

I stepped up to the limo. The moon roof was open. "Been stargazing?" I asked her.

"Actually, I wanted to make sure the two of you wouldn't be shot and thrown in the South China Sea. The last thing we need is a foreign government swarming this island with agents. If that happens, every bad person will crawl into a hole, and we will never be able to cut the head off Viper."

Her assessment was valid, to a degree. "Duly noted. But results matter. And we pulled it off without a confrontation." Her mouth opened, but I quickly filled the dead air. "Hey, we can still use this view to see when Shek leaves in the Mercedes. He might go straight home, or he might make take another side trip."

"Commander, Mr. Whitfield…"

I stared at Jet. "You call her Commander?"

"It's kind of a joke, but not really. She's got a commanding presence." He gave her a finger wave. She rolled her eyes, then motioned with her hand for him to share his thought.

"Did you see that crate next to Spike?"

I quickly checked my pictures, but they were closeups of Shek and his two associates. Not much of the periphery. Spike was off-camera to the right. "There was a crate?"

"Doesn't matter, because I took care of everything."

Su jammed her hands onto her hips. "What did you do now, Jet?"

Jet's teeth glowed, and then his phone glowed, which showed off his dancing eyebrows. "Commander, did I ever tell you that I developed my own personal app for a tracking device I made?"

I pointed at Jet. "Did you…?"

"Damn straight I did."

20

Macau Jockey Club
Taipa

The limo's windshield wipers scraped the glass every few seconds. It felt like they were scraping the back of my eyeballs.

"Jack, you forced my hand. I had no choice," Su said.

I ignored her. "Jet, any movement on the tracker?"

"Hold on. I had to reboot my phone. Gotta remember that the app is still in beta."

We were sitting in a convenience store parking lot—the store was closed for the night—one street south of the Macau Jockey Club. The black Mercedes, with Shek and Spike, had traveled into Taipa and entered the horse-racing facility, according to the tracker that Jet had affixed to the crate. With the place nothing more than a ghost town, there was no way for us to follow and blend in with a nonexistent crowd.

I scratched my face and tried not to take out my agitation on anyone. Well, at least not my full wrath. In some respects, we still had reason to be optimistic that this night would provide evidence of Shek's specific involvement with Viper, thanks to Jet's ingenuity and daring act back at the Full Moon Marina. Brilliant and risky at the same time.

Once Jet had shared the good news, there wasn't much time to celebrate or to plot next moves. Within a minute of Jet's revelation, Spike and Shrek had loaded the crate into the trunk of the Mercedes and pulled out of the marina parking lot. The other two men had hopped on a speedboat.

My idea had been to grab a boat from my old buddy Tom so I could follow them. In a parallel effort, Su and Jet could follow the crate. Divide and conquer, I'd told them.

That was when our team started to crack at the seams.

Su shot down the idea, saying it was far too risky for me navigate dark, foreign waters on my own. I didn't want to hear it. She didn't want to have to babysit me. We argued until the clock ran out—the two associates were long gone in their speedboat, as were Shek and Spike in the Mercedes

"Are you still upset with me?" Su rested her hand on mine, and I it jerked away.

"You only did this because we're on your turf. If this had been in the—" I clipped my comment, knowing I'd already spoken too much.

"The United States, perhaps?"

I shook my head.

There was a ding, and Su brought her phone to eye level. Wondering if the MSS already had processed the photos and come back with intel on Shek's two acquaintances, I tried to read the message, but she had some type of privacy screen over the face of the phone.

I checked my phone, but Simon hadn't yet responded. I tapped the front seat. "Any movement on the crate, Jet?"

"Okay, they entered the facility on the northeast side. According to my app, they're still in the same vicinity. And just so you know, as long as we're within two miles, I can track the device to within ten feet of its actual position."

I turned to Su, who was gazing out the window, a thousand-yard stare. "Did your handler get back to you on Shek's marina buddies?" I asked.

She glanced at me, then back to the window. The view was the wall that bordered the horse-racing facility. I waited her out.

"Only an update from home," she said with little energy. "How about you?"

"Nothing on my end either." I scratched my face, the stubble like wire. "Jet, any idea what was in the crate?"

He shook his head.

Su spoke up. "No evidence of ice on or around the crate? It could have just been some fish."

"I was too nervous to inspect it much. Didn't want Spike to pound me."

"Any words or logos on the crate?" Su pressed.

"Didn't see any." Jet shot upright in his driver's seat. "We've got movement."

"Where?" Su and I said in tandem.

"Have they left the facility?" I asked.

He moved his eyes up and then back to the screen. "They're headed our way."

"They're what?"

Jet's head bounced up and down. "Yup. From inside the facility. They're headed right for us."

I shot a look at Su. "Where could they be going?"

Su motioned for Jet to show her the phone screen. He did. She said, "This has no map of the facility."

"It's not Google Earth, if that's what you're asking. It's a bit crude."

"What do you think, Su?" I asked.

"The buildings across the street from us hold supplies for the concession stands, food for the horses, old saddles, uniforms for the riders. Many things."

"Could be a drug stash," I said. "Maybe they use the club as some sort of distribution hub."

"Possible."

"Have you actually raced there?"

"I have been 'injured,'" she said, using air quotes.

"But you have access to the facility."

"Not those buildings."

"We need to figure out which building the crate is in."

"If they leave it there," Jet said.

"Good point. They could be meeting someone. Someone who works for the club."

"Possible," Su said.

I opened my car door. "Jet, I need you to boost me up to the roof of one of those buildings over there."

"But you—"

"Stop, Su. I can't sit back and just wait and see. If there's anyone with Shek and Spike, we need to know who it is. And we need to verify which building the crate is in."

"If they leave it there," Jet said again.

"True. Maybe I'll be able to see as much from the roof. I don't know. But I'll be discreet."

Su shook her head. "I do not like this, Jack."

I didn't bother arguing her use of my real name. "You don't have a choice this time."

21

Macau Jockey Club
Taipa

Jet and I scooted into a small alley that separated buildings one and two, bordering the south side of the facility. Using Jet's app, we estimated that the crate—and hopefully Shek and his contact at the club—were somewhere near or inside building three.

From my standing position in the alley, the flat rooftop had to be at least fifteen feet up.

"I should go," Jet said. "I'm younger, more agile. Plus, since I'm Chinese, no one would be surprised to see me."

"On a roof? I don't think your ethnicity will help much."

"But I can speak Cantonese and talk my way out of it."

He had me on that one. But I'd never relied on others to carry out tasks that were mine alone. Especially not when the lives of my wife and daughter were on the line.

"If either of us is caught up there by the wrong people, our language won't help a damn bit." We'd also draw the ire of Su, which might be just as unpleasant. Better left unsaid. For now, Su had agreed to stay in the car and keep an eye out for potential threats, on foot or in a vehicle.

Jet interlocked his beefy fingers. I stepped into the human webbing, pushed up, and… I smacked my nose against the stucco, my hand about a foot below the roof of building two. "Down, down," I said.

I dropped to the alley and huffed out a breath.

"Ready for me to give it a try?" Jet asked. "I can do it. I can be your eyes on the roof."

"Why are you doing all this for Su?"

"I came to Macau for an exciting adventure, but the casinos turned out not to be that exciting. And then I met Su. No way I'll do anything for the Chinse government, but working with her has given me a purpose. It's all that and a bag of chips."

"Okay. Well, after you help boost me up, you can monitor the blinking red dot in your app from the safe confines of the limo."

Jet didn't argue—a miracle.

I altered our method for getting me on the roof. Four steps to gain momentum. One step into Jet's hand-stirrup. I grabbed the ledge with one hand but quickly started to slip. My other hand took hold. Steady, steady …

"Got it?" Jet asked.

I didn't. Not in the least. Both hands slipped on loose pebbles, and I frantically tried to brush the pebbles aside until my fingers caught more traction. On the verge of falling, my fingertips managed to grab the concrete lip, and I pulled myself up with a fair amount of grunting and cursing. Once on the roof, I gave Jet a thumbs-up, and he scurried back to the limo.

The surface of the roof was pebbled tar, wet and slick. With ambient lighting from a few streetlights, my field of vision was adequate. There was a large air conditioning unit and a few vents and pipes sticking through the rooftop.

I dropped down and bear-crawled across building two.

The most dangerous part of this operation was just ahead—leaping to building three. Jet had said as much, and so had Su. In fact, she'd warned me twice not to attempt it. But she didn't know about my track background.

As a decathlete at the University of Tennessee, I'd set the record for most points in the Southeastern Conference and went on to compete in international meets throughout the world. My crowning achievement was qualifying for the US Olympic team, but a freak injury forced me to watch my teammates compete. While I'd always wondered what my life would be like had I not pulled a hamstring, I never once regretted the world I shared with Anna and Maddie. They were the heartbeat of my life. My everything.

I heard voices coming from the front of building three. I peeked over the edge. A glow from below. Headlights. Possibly the Mercedes that held the crate. I edged nearer to the corner but couldn't get close enough to see the people on the ground.

As I pulled back from the edge, I noticed a large mound of sand on the ground. Probably to fill the track on the inside loop.

It was about a fifteen-foot jump to the roof of building three. In normal circumstances—in daylight, on a dry surface, with the proper footwear and athletic clothes—I was capable of jumping twenty feet. Maybe more with my adrenaline kicking in. But I was keenly aware of the risks. I didn't have a chance to pace out my steps and do any dry runs to ensure I'd hit the takeoff mark at the optimum point. The lack of lighting hurt my depth perception, which could impact my takeoff and landing. And the lack of traction—inadequate shoes and a wet surface. If these conditions were at an actual track meet, my college coach would insist on postponing the event.

I didn't have that luxury. I had one shot to make it to the other side.

"Let's do this." I spat into both hands and rubbed them together, the same routine I'd carried out at track meets.

I pushed out of my stance, pumping my arms while trying to get a read on where my launch foot should plant for takeoff. Five steps before the rooftop ended, I could see the edge of darkness from below. Not something I was accustomed to.

I blocked all doubt from my mind and focused on hitting the last step with momentum and balance.

An explosive exhale. My body airborne. Arms and legs pulling at the nighttime air. Propelling me forward.

I landed.

I'd cleared the alley by at least two feet, my weight out in front of me. I rolled twice until my shoulder was stopped cold by a pipe.

Nothing broken. I brushed pebbles off my side as I got to my feet and walked cautiously toward the front of the rooftop.

Voices again. Garbled Cantonese. I almost called Jet and Su to see if they could interpret, but I knew they'd have a difficult time hearing the conversation. I tiptoed closer. One man had a distinct accent, possibly British or Australian. It was animated. I wanted to move up to the very edge so I could hear better, maybe see something, but I didn't want to risk getting caught.

The AC unit. I crawled on top of it and moved up to my knees to get a visual. I saw spears of gelled hair—the top of Spike's head.

My phone buzzed, but I ignored it. A beat of silence and I held my breath. Then just as quickly, the conversation continued as before. I lifted my phone, inches away from capturing this new player in a picture. And maybe see the contents of what was inside the crate. I slowly rose to standing.

A spotlight swept over me. "Você está preso!" *You're under arrest!*

I jerked my sights toward the street. Two cops, one with a gun aimed right at me, the other shining a spotlight. My phone. It must have been Su or Jet warning me the cops were close by.

My mind started spinning. I had no way out. Thugs on one side, cops on the other. And the cops would probably soon multiply. I wasn't a simple trespasser. I was a foreigner using a fake identity. I'd be branded a spy by the Chinese. The fact that Macau was a special administrative region would have no bearing on how they would treat me. The US government would play ignorant, because they were. All hope to reunite with Anna and Maddie would be lost. What more would Simon do to them while I rotted in a Macau jail?

I ran to the side of the rooftop, skidding to a stop just before the edge. I looked down, contemplated jumping to the alley beneath me. The cops were only forty feet away, lights and sirens everywhere. I backtracked to the east side of the roof. The distance to building four seemed even greater than the one on the west side. And it would buy me nothing. The cops would only need to shift their positions a few yards. I could hide on the roof. But they would eventually figure out a way up. I still had my gun… I needed wings, though, not weaponry.

A memory broke through the mayhem. Something I'd seen just a few minutes ago—the large mound of sand. The idea was nuts. I might break a leg. My back. My head. Or all that and more. But it was the only chance I had to stay free.

I pulled my gun from my holster and hid it next to the AC unit. I couldn't afford it going off and firing into my foot. Then I turned to the front of the building, and using the backdrop of the club's grandstand, I got my bearings. Mentally calibrated the angle and force I'd need to use.

For Anna. For Maddie.

I ran toward the front edge of the roof and jumped with

everything I had.

22

My adrenaline got the best of me, and I lost my balance midair—my weight way over the top of my feet. I hit the mound of packed sand with less of a thud than I'd imagined. But gravity was just starting to play its wicked game. My body was hurled beyond the mound like a bowling ball. My teeth clapped together, my limbs feeling like they were being detached from their sockets, my head bouncing repeatedly off the ground.

I'd been a world-class decathlete, competed at the highest levels of human competition in meets across the globe, but I'd never been so physically punished in a single three-second span.

When I finally stopped, I tried to inhale. Couldn't. I tried again. Still no air. My lungs weren't working.

Shouting all around me, but I didn't care. My lungs couldn't take in air. Not even a little bit. Panic started to set in. I rubbed my torso, thumped my chest. No joy. What the hell was going on?

My eyes bulged. Angry voices grew closer. Would they see

my panic and help me?

More likely, kill me.

A recollection from third grade popped to the forefront of my mind. Me sitting on the soles of Big Dave's feet so he could launch me into the air. Up I went, and I saw the top of the basketball rim for the first time. I landed on my tailbone and couldn't regain my breathing. My lung had collapsed. After a panicked two minutes, Dave picked me up and dropped me on my ass. My lung unfolded.

Back to the here and now. My brain felt like a water balloon about to pop. I had to take action. I lifted my butt up and dropped back to the ground.

Jarred brain. Still no air.

If there was a state of mind beyond panic, I was in it. Seconds from drowning—without the water. Legs shuffled somewhere in my periphery. If Spike or someone else killed me, it would only end the absolute misery.

Using every ounce of my remaining energy, I jumped three, maybe four feet off the ground. Then I thrust myself downward with aggression.

The extreme force of the landing rippled up my spine.

And I coughed.

I coughed again and again. I heaved in a beautiful, full breath.

"Oh God," I muttered, rolling to my side.

A shadow crossed my space. I looked up.

Spike grunting, thrashing something at me. I rolled. A metal pipe smacked my calf. Stung like hell, but it didn't hit bone. I was still mobile. Up to my knees, and he lunged for me. I grabbed a handful of sand and tossed it at his eyes. He whelped, his body moving, but the arm holding the pipe dropped to his side as he struggled to clear his eyes. I stuck out my foot, and he tripped, face-planting into the mound of sand.

I glanced over my shoulder. Shek and another person in silhouette. A woman. They were walking toward me. Guns? I couldn't tell.

More sirens and whistles and voices from the other side of the wall that encompassed the jockey club. Macau police.

I flipped on my heels and ran toward the track, zigzagging as I went. Hoping to stay one step ahead of a bullet.

A pinging sound, and I quickly checked body parts. Missed me. Seeking the cover of darkness, I crossed the grass track, the sand track, and jumped over the railing. The stagnant pond to my left glowed as if it were filled with nuclear waste. In this part of the world, anything was possible.

I curled around the water and hid behind a small building surrounded by six-foot trees. Panting like a dog in the heat of the Smoky Mountains in July. I peeked around the corner, and no one was chasing after me. Not yet. But the buildings were awash in light. The police could have scaled the wall and were now on the inside of the facility.

I scanned the area for the best escape route. So many options, but officers could be positioned at every one of them. They knew this place, probably had a map. Not me. I didn't know a damn…

Su and Jet! There was hope. I pulled out my phone.

Shards of glass sprinkled into my hand. The phone was dead. Useless.

Voices over a megaphone, so close I could feel it in my ribcage. I took three steps from the cover of the trees and hurled my phone into the middle of the pond. No finding it there.

Keeping the cover of the small building and trees behind me, I raced across the north side of the track, first the sand and then the grass. Stayed low to the ground. Hustle, hustle, hustle. I crossed in front of the grandstand, heading for the front gates, then passed the winner's circle. A platform, dark mulch, a large metal tub for horses to drink water. I needed water.

Moving on. I took three steps and stopped. A man was just up ahead, looking toward the commotion on the south side of the facility. He was swinging a chain. No idea if that was his only weapon or with whom he was aligned. And there could be more right behind him.

Shifting to the side of the grandstand, I paused and tried to come up with a new escape route.

White lights bounced across the infield. Macau police officers were headed my way. No time for debate. With my options now much more limited, I ran behind the grandstand, looking for a way out. Another gate. A hole in the wall, whatever. No such luck. I did locate an exit gate, but it had razor wire looped over the top.

Jogging along the fence line, I looked for a gap. Whistles echoed all around me. If officers were waiting on the outside of this north fence, it would not end well for me.

I stopped at a small building, some type of concession stand, and craned my neck, looking upward.

The roof of the building was almost equal to the height of the razor wire just behind it. And then about another fifteen-foot drop to concrete. It was an insane idea. But it was the only idea at the moment, so I took it. I shimmied up the building's downspout, praying the gutter wouldn't break away from the siding.

I reached the roof, exhausted. Sucking fumes. But there was more work to do. If I took this leap and didn't break my ankle or my neck, I wanted to believe I'd be home free. Or free for now.

No sign of Spike or police officers. When I faced the fence, I noticed a small tree planted in the middle of the sidewalk on the other side. Beyond that, the LRT and towering office buildings.

I hurled myself over the fence and razor wire, landing in the foliage. The weak, leafy branches punctured my skin, but they also cushioned my fall. I'd take abrasions over broken bones.

And certainly over collapsed lungs.

I heaved out a breath. The tree may have saved my ass, but I still wasn't safe. I raced down the sidewalk in search of a hiding spot and water.

23

Taipa

Hiding in a small cove next to a tall building near an LRT station, I pulled a train pass from my pocket, the same one I'd used earlier in the night. Felt like a month ago. It would be my ticket out of harm's way. Assuming, of course, the cops hadn't already thought of that.

I couldn't afford to stay in this spot for long. Police officers were scouring the confines of the jockey club. While it was a large facility with countless hiding spots, eventually they would expand their search.

A distant siren reverberated off the surrounding concrete and stone. It was so loud I covered my ears. And then it stopped.

A police car drove past my location. No siren and no lights. Also, no noise. An electric car. It was moving so slowly I could see the two officers scanning left and right. Looking for someone.

Me.

My cotton mouth turned into a desert as I stood stock-still. I hoped my position in the shadows wasn't visible from the road. The car moved at only five or ten miles per hour, rolling past me without incident. But the longer I stayed there, the more likely I'd get caught.

I glanced at the LRT station. No train. I recalled a tree-filled hill on the other side of the building. I'd be safe there for a short period of time at least.

I stepped out of the cove, and the police car stopped just down the road. Another officer ran up from inside the club fence and shouted to the driver, who had his window down. Not a good sign. This place could be swarming with cops within minutes. Maybe less.

I pulled back into the cover of darkness but kept an eye on the car and the officer at the fence. Perhaps someone had seen me scale that roof and jump over the fence. I could make it to the hill on the other side of the building in just seconds. I could do it.

A furious roar. I glanced upward. An LRT train. The rumble grew louder and then died back as brakes squealed at the jockey club station. For a brief moment, I pictured myself racing up the staircase and jumping on the train just before the doors shut. But that was pure fantasy. The distance from my position to the train was probably north of a hundred yards—up two flights of stairs, no less. The trains probably stopped for no more than thirty seconds. Even in my Olympic days, it would have taken a record-breaking effort. At the age of thirty-six, dehydrated, and barely recovered from my last beating, I had no chance.

People exited the train, meandered down the stairs, along the sidewalk—right in front of me.

I could blend.

I eyeballed the cops in the distance. One glanced in my general direction, then went back to talking to his colleagues.

"Here goes everything." I stepped out onto the sidewalk just behind two ladies and began walking with them, in the opposite direction of the officers.

No yelling. No whistles. So far so good.

I kept my head down, my hands in my pockets. About fifty feet later, I veered into an alley and kept walking. The faint outline of the steep hills was just up ahead.

It was time to turn into a goat.

24

Unknown location

Anna awoke to the sound of loud voices outside their room. At least two, likely more. None had the same timber as the man with the limp.

Her body tensed, and she moved to her knees while keeping a hand on Maddie—she was still sleeping. A miracle.

Anna listened more closely for specific words, a clue about their fate. A voice rose above the others, but she couldn't understand a single word. The man spoke some dialect of Chinese. Dread rippled through her body. Confirmation that they were likely somewhere in China, a nation of 1.4 billion people. While some components of the society were advanced, the communist government cared little for human rights, still less for women. Even worse, Anna knew of seedier elements that operated under the radar, kidnapping and trafficking girls from countries that rimmed the South China Sea—Vietnam, the

Philippines, and others.

She couldn't swallow—her throat had shut just like that time when she was a kid and she'd been bitten by a dozen bees. The promise of being reunited with Jack after his bizarre mission could have been a ruse to keep her and Maddie calm. She had to face a grim reality. Jack might not know their location. Hell, he might not even be alive, despite her being told otherwise.

Had she and Maddie just been sold to the highest bidder? She searched the corners of the room. No cameras were visible, but that didn't mean they weren't being watched.

A lock unlatched, and the door creaked open.

"I have your meal." The man with a limp, who always wore a surgical mask, set the tray on the floor. "It may not be five-star food, but my mom told me to appreciate three squares a day." He looked at the tray, then at Anna. "Or maybe two squares."

"Where are you from?" Anna asked.

He studied her a second. "I shouldn't give you specific information. Let's just say the United States. It's a big country with lots of people, right?" he said with a chuckle.

"Yep. A real melting pot." She reached over and tried to use her fingers to pick up some of stew on the plate.

"Kind of messy, huh?"

"Yeah."

He pulled a napkin from his pocket and gave it to her.

"Thanks."

He peered into the hallway—she looked around him but saw only darkness—then he turned back toward her. "You ain't going anywhere."

"We're not? I mean, we'll leave when Jack finishes that important mission, right?"

"Right. You sure will. Anyway…" He pulled a plastic fork from his pocket, dropping it on the tray. "You don't need to be eating like an animal."

"Thank you. I've been trying to teach Maddie how to use a fork, so this is helpful."

"No problem." He turned and left.

Anna emptied her lungs. It didn't appear that she and Maddie were about to be hauled away to the highest bidder. There was at least a little bit of time to act. She rubbed Maddie's back while eyeing the plastic fork.

A plan began to formulate.

25

Halfway up the hillside, I'd already encountered rough terrain, and a piece of bamboo stabbing my socked foot—my shoe had slipped off. This was as good a place to rest as any, and I fell onto my back, breathing hard. Concealed amongst trees, thick brush, and bamboo shoots, I tried to calm my nerves. I'd been lucky as hell so far, surviving jumps, falls, beatings, and a manhunt. While the bamboo had won a small battle, I was winning the war.

From my vantage point, I could see part of the jockey club between two tall buildings. Myriad dots of light bounced around the infield—their hunt had intensified. Didn't these people have bigger problems to address?

I blew out a lungful of air and put my shoe back on.

I thought about Shek and Spike, and the mystery person who spoke with an Australian accent. And the silhouette of the woman. If there really was something illegal in that storage unit or the crate, what better way to distract officers than to throw all the focus onto me? The notorious foreign terrorist or whatever.

Even if I was a wanted man for make-believe crimes, it didn't change my purpose.

A wrenching anguish seared my soul as I thought about my family. Damn, I'd do anything to have Anna and Maddie here with me. Yes, even on this Macau hillside in the middle of the night. I could picture Maddie sitting on my leg and pretending to steal my nose. She loved to play the game, giggling the entire time. Once she started to giggle, her battery lasted forever.

Her infectious giggle.

And Anna. *Oh, my Anna.*

I would make things as right as I could. They would not break me.

I longed to go solo and just do my own thing, but I couldn't pull off this mission without support. I had no phone and no access to Simon—my only connection to my wife and daughter. Su and Jet were still my best source for information.

Just days ago, I would never have dreamed of being where I was today, this moment. But despite the setbacks, my yearning to finish this mission successfully and reunite with my family was more intense than any feeling I'd ever known.

I would find Su and Jet. Get a new phone. Drill for info on the trafficking operations.

Rescue Cai Chen.

I would succeed. No question about it.

26

Ritz-Carlton Hotel
Cotai

A small weight on my chest as I slept. A dream? The real thing? I tried to crack open one eye, but every part of my body ached. Even my eye sockets.

I recalled walking into my room late in the night, surprised to see a replacement phone, and an additional backup, courtesy of Simon. The pain from the bone-shattering leap off the building. I had craved relief that only a pill could bring. Still, somehow, I fell asleep.

Something smacked the mattress, and I shot upright, my cell phone slipping from my chest.

"Su?" A second later, I was bathed in blinding light. "What the hell are you doing?"

"I cannot believe what you have put us through, Jack. And now you are in here just sleeping."

"Can you do something about the light?"

I heard curtains sliding shut, and the penetrating glare disappeared.

"Thanks." I dragged my feet over the side of the bed and used the heel of my hand to wipe my eyes, clear the mental cobwebs. It didn't help much. I rotated my arm; my shoulder socket hurt like hell. Everything hurt like hell. I released a long groan.

"Did you get drunk or something?"

"Are you crazy? I was looking for you and Jet, and then—"

"But I found you."

I splayed my arms. "That's what I was going to say. Since my old phone was destroyed, I had no way to contact you. I figured you'd eventually check my room."

She sat in a chair in the corner. "I see you already have a new phone. Your handler moves quickly."

"Will you stop with that? I don't have a handler. I'm a..." I didn't bother to finish. I was too sore. "You got any pain meds on you, or can you get me some? I'm dying here."

She shook her head and stood up, quickly dismissing me. "For some odd reason, the MSS is having a difficult time retrieving further details about the real you. But you could end the mystery by telling me right now." She leaned in.

Part of me wanted to tell someone, just to relieve the mental burden. But she wasn't just someone. She was an agent for China's main intelligence agency. Even if she said her prime motivation for this mission was personal—getting Ubaldo out of the Triad—she was still a trained agent. I'd been warned by Simon not to trust anyone. The battle raged within me. Trust Simon? Trust Su? If I appealed to her softer side and shared my real story, could she help. But would she?

I decided not to make a decision and shifted topics. "How did you get into my room?"

She smiled.

"Oh, right," I scoffed. "Your real job."

"You probably have the same skills, Jack, even if you come across as a little naïve."

I let silence be my answer, and I walked to the bathroom sink and doused my face with water.

"After I checked on you about an hour ago," Su said, "I took a power nap, then showered and changed. I'm ready to go."

I wiped my face with a towel. Su was wearing black bodycon jeans and a crisp gold shirt.

"You were in here earlier? You're a machine. I'm trying to scoop up my brain right now."

"You look like shit."

"Feel like it. Could feel better if you would only get me some damn—"

"Just glad you made it back without being arrested," she said, once again ignoring my plea for pain relief. Probably for the best. "Even though Macau is a special administrative region, it is still part of China. Getting you out of jail would be messy for all parties, including your home country."

She asked if I'd seen anything noteworthy from the rooftop at the club. I noted the man with the accent and the mystery woman.

"I almost got a picture, just before the cops spotted me. After that, it was all downhill." I chugged some water, which seemed to lubricate the gears in my mind. "Where's Jet? Actually, where's the crate?"

"Jet is keeping an eye on the crate through his app. It is stationary, in that building at the jockey club. He will let me know if it is on the move." She waggled her cell phone. "Jack, I cannot believe you jumped off that building. Your neck could have been broken, or worse."

"Eh."

"Your ability to act under duress, to survive these physical challenges, is unlike almost any I have witnessed. I am impressed. Someone has trained you well. The question is: who?"

Enough about me. "Okay, what's next?"

"Get dressed." She tossed a pair of trousers at me. "Ubaldo says he has intel to share."

27

Senado Square
Macau

A car backfired on the busy road just behind us, and I startled.

"You are jumpy," Su said. "But I get it. You had a rough night." She smiled and turned to gaze at a display window full of colorful hats, then continued to stroll on by.

I was beginning to understand some of Su's nuances in her body language. When she marched, it was all business. And no one wanted to be on the receiving end of whatever she was about to deliver. Right now, she walked with an easy, casual gait. She was Tourist Su. I'd come to the conclusion that this parallel universe of hidden truths and buried lies was ingrained in her DNA. Maybe the Chinese had somehow mastered a way to actually make that happen. For me, I was just faking it one act at a time.

We skirted around a sidewalk artist painting a boat in a dark harbor. "Where's this place we're meeting Ubaldo?" I asked.

"Just beyond St. Dominic's Church. Follow the wavy lines."

The beige and purple wavy lines were actually thousands of tiny tiles that served as the road and walkway in Senado Square, where the Portuguese culture was out in full force. If you stared at the wavy lines long enough, it did a number on your vision. So, I kept my sights up and searched the crowd for Ubaldo.

As the walkway narrowed, there was the rustic, gold façade of a church on the left. Across the street was a café that specialized in coffee, one of dozens of coffee houses in Macau.

"I don't see him."

"Please be patient, Jack. Remember what Ubaldo told me."

Ubaldo's phone call to Su had been quick but worrisome. Ubaldo had called Su from a dry-cleaning business, the first sign something wasn't right. He went on to say that Liou, the leader of the Y2K Triad, had ordered all members to turn in their cell phones at the start of last night's shift. Ubaldo had heard through the rumor mill that Liou was worried about someone leaking information. If Liou had solid evidence of betrayal, death was a certainty for the perpetrator, according to Ubaldo. Even though his phone had been returned to him at the end of the shift, it was clear that everyone was under suspicion.

"You think someone might be following him?" My eyes scanned the crowd through dark sunglasses.

"It is possible. But Ubaldo is a savvy kid. He will make sure, as best he can, that he is not followed."

Her words were confident, but her tone was not.

We walked into the open-air coffee shop, ordered two iced teas, and found a small table under the canopy.

A distant chant snagged my attention, and I shot Su a questioning look.

"Protestors," she said before sipping her drink.

"For…?"

"I figured you would be keenly aware of the anti-government protestors, Jack."

I recalled seeing pictures of Chinese police using tear gas on protestors. Another reminder that citizens in this country didn't have the same freedoms as those in the US, or even in England. "This is Macau. I thought the fight was about freedom in Hong Kong."

"It is spreading. Since Macau is a special administrative region like Hong Kong, people are voicing a similar warning."

"I hadn't really thought about it much since I arrived. Been blinded by all the money. But I guess freedom is something I've always taken for granted. What do you think?" I asked.

"About what?"

"Do you support the protestors?"

She pursed her lips. "I understand their cause."

Seemed like she was riding the fence, or simply didn't want to give away her position. "What are they chanting?"

"'Step down, Xela.' And 'Xela is a traitor to her people.'"

"Who's that?"

"The chief administrator of Macau. Some people believe she is just a puppet to Beijing."

"Are you part of the 'some people'?"

Before she could reply, a young man pulled out the third chair at our table and sat down.

I lifted my sunglasses. "Wen?"

"Where's Ubaldo?" Su asked.

"I'm thirsty." He glanced over my shoulder, presumably at the menu above the front counter.

"Wen, I am not joking." Su's voice was on the rise. I touched her forearm, and she gave me a stern look.

"We just want answers, not to draw attention to ourselves," I said.

She gave me an eye nod, then returned her focus to Wen,

who was now leaning his chair back on two legs. He and I had a history, and I wondered if this surprise visit was somehow connected to it.

Su cleared her throat and spoke in a calm manner. "Can you tell us where Ubaldo is?"

"Busy doing something for Liou," he said with a lift of his chin. "He asked me to meet up with you and share this new information he has learned."

Su tapped a finger to the table, and Wen dropped his chair to all four legs. "What is the message?"

"You are not even going to offer to buy me a drink?" he asked with a cocky chuckle.

"What can I get you?" I started to stand, but Su grabbed my arm.

"Drink after you talk," she said to Wen. "What did Ubaldo want to share with us?"

"You're a ball-buster, lady." He leaned on the table with his forearms and lowered his voice. "If you want to see what this show is all about, you need to check out Rob's party."

"Rob?"

"Robinson. Arthur Robinson, right?" I said.

He looked at me, shaking his head. "I am not talking to you. You murdered my brother."

A few heads turned in our direction. I couldn't afford this to escalate. "I told you—"

Su nudged my forearm, shifting her sights to the kid. "Wen, we know you are hurting about the death of your brother. But we also know why that happened. Clayton was defending himself."

"But—"

She held up a finger, stopping his protest. "Wen, this is why I want to get you and Ubaldo out of the Triad. It infects your mind. You will see the world differently once you are free from crime, from thinking like a thug."

He clapped out a laugh full of contempt. "Free? We will never be free, lady."

Normally, I wouldn't have much patience for a kid like Wen. But behind his brash attitude was someone in pain. I'd give him the benefit of the doubt, but only to a point. My mission would not be derailed by him or anyone else.

Su clasped her hands on the table. "Tell me about this party by Mr. Robinson."

"Never been to one," Wen said, his eyes everywhere but on Su or me.

"But there's a reason why Ubaldo said to check out the party, right?" I pressed.

Wen scoffed—arrogant attitude still front and center. "You must be dense or something," he said. "Let me spell it out for you. It is where the rich party, no holds barred, man. All the drugs free of charge. Girls too. Plenty of girls. I've heard stories that would… Well, I will just leave it at that."

I smacked the table. "Like what? What have you heard? And where are the girls kept?"

Wen looked at Su, pointed at me. "I will not talk to him."

Su's knee touched mine under the table. Somehow, I withstood the urge to grab Wen and shake him until he told me everything.

"What else do you know about the girls?" Su asked.

"Nothing, really," Wen said. "Just heard stories about these raves."

"Do you know when the next one is scheduled?"

"Tonight. That is why I'm here."

"When can Ubaldo reach out to me?"

"I'm not his mother. He said he told you."

"Told me what?"

"The spooks are out. People are watching and talking. This whole damn thing is so messed up. No way out." Wen shook his head as his gaze dropped to the floor.

Su placed the palms of her hands on the table. “You know my goal, Wen. I want to blow up this entire operation. So you and Ubaldo can finally rid yourselves of this corrosive group and do something good for yourself. And think about how many people will be saved from drug addiction, all the girls who will gain their freedom. This can happen. But we need help.”

Wen’s eyes shifted to me, and his jaw clenched. A brief stare-down, then he turned back to Su. “I told you the info from Ubaldo. I have done my part, and now I am out of here.”

He pushed back the chair, making a loud scraping sound, and then disappeared into the crowd.

28

Penha Hill, Macau

Sitting in the back of a Honda Stepwagon Spada—Jet said he used the minivan for "operations"—I rubbed my bare chin and watched Jet through the side window. "It's been at least a minute. You think his buddy, Ricardo, might be rethinking the deal?"

When Su didn't immediately respond, I glanced in her direction. She was busy reading a message on her phone.

"What's so important?"

"Received intel back on Shek's two associates from the marina." She stowed her phone in a small clutch and peered out the window.

"And?"

No response.

My phone then buzzed with a message. I read it, slipped the phone into my pocket. Went back to looking out the window.

"What was that about?" she asked.

"I just received intel back on Shek's two associates from the marina," I deadpanned.

She narrowed her eyes. "Enough with the games, Jack Whitfield."

"I'm not joking." I summarized the text from Simon. "The Anglo is an Australian national. Has captained several ships running illegal cargo throughout Southeast Asia. Goes by the name Sly. The second guy is a dangerous criminal named Liou Changming."

"The head of the Y2K Triad. But what I find interesting is that you received your intel at virtually the same time as me."

I was also intrigued. Actually, I was stunned. Were Simon and the Chinese MSS connected? My mind took two mental leaps forward to my next internal question: could Simon actually be part of the MSS? Uncorking the implications, if that were true, nearly sent my mind into a tailspin.

"Look. Jet has the package," Su said.

The car door opened, and Jet placed a box on the passenger seat.

"What was the holdup?" Su asked him.

He huffed out a breath and pinched the corners of his eyes.

"Jet, are you worried he might try to alert Robinson's people about us posing as caterers for this party?"

"Nothing like that," he said, dejected, staring blankly at the grocery store parking lot.

"What's the deal, then?" I asked as I situated the box between Su and me. I started shuffling through the contents to make sure everything was there.

"I used to date Ricardo's cousin."

I stopped sifting through the box and glanced at Su, who picked up the baton. "What are you trying to say, Jet? We need to know if there is even a small chance we could be compromised."

"Nothing like that. Ricardo didn't ask questions. He doesn't care. But he did make me promise that I take his cousin out on a date."

"It's just one date. Can't be that bad," I said.

He eyed me through his rearview mirror. "Last time I tried to break it off, she tried to stab my you-know-what."

I snorted out a laugh. "Wear a steel cup."

Su held up the formal catering outfit. "We need to meet the other workers at the guest gate in twenty minutes. Time to get dressed."

"I'm walking around the parking lot while you two…" Jet waggled his fingers at us. "Do your thing." He exited the vehicle.

Before I could ask what he was talking about, Su pulled her shirt over her head. She wasn't wearing a bra.

"Do not be a prude, Jack. Now turn around. The peep show is over."

29

Robinson Estate
Penha Hill, Macau

A bus motored past us, blowing leaves and sand in the faces of the thirty or so employees of Top Flight Catering. A few squealed, some coughed, including me, but Su was unfazed.

"That didn't bother you?" I asked in a gravelly voice.

"Focusing."

I guess that's a no.

A man walked through the crowd and reminded us how important it was to be professional tonight. "Some of you will be enticed by what you see. Some of you may be repulsed. Do not let either of those emotions dictate your actions. We cannot and will not allow our employees to become part of the event or to protest that event. We do the job, and then we clean up and leave. Is that understood?"

Nods and verbal affirmations all around. We understood.

As we got in line behind the catering vans, I adjusted my vest.

"Do not fidget with your button," Su said.

She was talking about the third button on my vest. "Didn't know I was." When I brought my hands together, I accidentally tapped the top of my ring. "I think your friends in Beijing just got a shot of your backside."

Su's handler had provided some crafty hi-tech support. A tiny camera—nothing more than a thin piece of cellophane film—was affixed to a button on each of our vests. Whenever we wanted to take a snapshot, we tapped the rings they'd given us to wear. We could then review the pictures later from Su's cell phone.

She eyed me. "Time to be on your A game."

"Just be careful."

"Says the man who jumps off buildings."

We each grabbed a bin and followed a procession of black-vested caterers down the brick steps leading to a six-car garage. My eyes stuck on the car closest to us, a black, futuristic sports car that looked like it was more suited for a 22nd-century Batman.

"A Bugatti La Voiture Noire," Su said. "Goes for twelve million US. They only sold one last year."

I shook my head. "This guy has more bloody money than—"

Su nudged me to move on, so I did. Down a corridor until we reached the fourth-floor kitchen, almost as large as the garage. One of two kitchens in the 17,000-square-foot mansion. We'd studied the floor plan earlier, courtesy of Simon. Of course, Simon didn't know I was working with an agent from MSS. At least, I didn't think they knew. I still wondered if the two organizations were somehow connected, or possibly one and the same.

While setting up the food and drink, I took note of the

intersection of styles, Asian and European. The countertops were made from green and pink marble. On the other side of the swinging kitchen door, there was a shadowbox hanging on the wall, featuring a crossbow with Asian characters etched in the background. A gold-embossed frame. Pillows and encased lanterns were off to the side.

The home was a colonial-style villa, the stucco exterior painted in pastel green. Not exactly a symbol of power. From a design standpoint, though—all power. The four-story Robinson mansion had more bedrooms and bathrooms than the White House, an indoor pool, an outdoor pool, countless balcony views, media rooms, wine cellars, and more.

Su was assigned to a bar station on the third floor. I made sure I was one of the serving crew. Best way to move through the various levels of the home. With a tray full of salmon salad rolls, I started my recon on the top floor, an open-air, modern setup. All clean lines, minimalist, fresh. I strolled through the crowd with a smile on my face and my entire being on high alert.

It was definitely a "rich people" party. Outfits and jewelry oozed money. What I found interesting was there were almost as many women as men in attendance. No sign of drugs or enslaved girls, though. Had Ubaldo received faulty information? I sure as hell hoped we weren't wasting our time.

I'd intended to roam all four floors on my first walkthrough, but I ran out of appetizers before finishing the open-air fourth floor. I grabbed another tray and made a beeline toward the fancy staircase to check in with Su. The steps were made of clear glass and were built into the middle of the main room on each floor.

Same party vibe on the third floor, just different décor. Antiques and books and conversation nooks. Not a single person stood out as suspicious or distressed.

What was I missing?

The night is young, I reminded myself. I kept moving.

Su gave me a nod as she poured champagne into flutes. No hidden signals there. I presumed that meant she hadn't seen anything out of the ordinary either. I grabbed two trays of salmon rolls and decided to explore the first and second floors. Same story as the fourth floor. Nothing stood out.

"Check out the view!" A woman with straight black hair grabbed my arm and pulled me onto a second-story balcony.

"Ma'am, I'm not allowed…" I stopped talking when I saw the view. The Macau Tower, which looked very similar to the Space Needle in Seattle, not only lit up the horizon, but also glowed across Sai Van Lake.

"That's just awesome, isn't it?"

When I glanced at the woman, I questioned whether she was old enough to be in high school, let alone drink. "It certainly is. Have you been to it?" I wanted to see if she truly had her freedom.

"Hell to the yeah. Daddy even let me bungee jump. Over seven hundred feet. It was frickin' awesome." She jumped up and down, finger-clapping.

That was my cue to reload the appetizers and do another run through the house.

I did a quick little bow and said, "Enjoy your time—"

"Oh, there's Daddy now. Hi, Daddy!"

I followed her gaze across the room to a man walking toward a hallway in the far corner. Though he never turned around, I knew that man.

It was Shek.

30

"Give me four drinks," I said to Su at the bar.

She shifted her eyes to the bartender, who was busy mixing some type of martini. "What would the guests like?" she asked, all business, professional.

"Uh, maybe…"

She nodded. "Right, four flutes of our finest champagne. Coming right up."

"Thanks. They're very thirsty, so…" I gave her a hurry-up roll of my hand. I didn't want to miss my chance. She finished the pours in no time.

I made it to the second-floor corridor where I'd last seen Shek, and one of the doors opened. I hurried in that direction and ran into a barrier. A human one.

"No entry," Spike said as he stepped into the hallway, quickly closing the door behind him.

I glanced away, worried he would recognize me.

"Do you hear me?" he asked.

"Sir, Mr. Shek Jian ordered four glasses of our finest champagne," I said, keeping my eyes to the ground. Maybe he'd think it was some sort of deferential servant move.

He grunted. "Hold on." Then he opened the door and walked inside.

I counted to ten but quickly lost patience, and my eyes began to roam. Saw another door. Walked up to it and heard loud voices, both male and female. I took a chance, turned the knob, and stepped inside.

Arthur Robinson, in a gold and red robe, snapped his fingers at me. "Champagne? You read my mind. Please…" He was surrounded by all types of women, a few clearly underage. To my left, behind a large privacy screen, the outline of people milling about, the din of their voices cheerful but subdued. I believed that was the room Spike had entered.

I walked closer to the massive bean bag chair upon which Robinson was lounging. When he reached up to grab the flute, he started to teeter over, his eyes fluttering. Two of the women helped him sit back up.

"I'm fine. I'm okay. No need to worry about old Arthur Robinson. Now, the champagne." When he leaned forward, his robe pulled apart some, exposing a large belly. "I saw you peeking," he said, popping his eyebrows.

"Me?" I tapped my chest.

Robinson flipped open his robe, then quickly closed it. "It's down there somewhere. You just have to shove all the belly fat out of the way." A throaty chuckle, and his entourage quickly joined in the laughter.

While the man was repulsive, I found myself staring at the two girls who obviously didn't belong. They were probably closer in age to Maddie than to me. Unfortunately, neither girl matched the picture I had of Cai Chen.

Robinson chugged the entire flute of champagne as though it

were water, finishing with an "*ahhh!*"

Unsure what to do with the three other glasses of champagne, I shuffled in place a few steps.

"Do you want to taste the fine Chinese cuisine, Mr. Waiter?" Robinson pulled the young girl wearing a pink halter top closer, sniffed her hair. She had no visible reaction, her eyes almost lifeless.

"I'm working, sir," I said.

He yanked her onto his lap and began to stroke her hair. "Oh, right. The hired help. I guess that means you don't have eyes and you don't have, uh…" He blinked rapidly, his head swaying for a few seconds. Finally, he snapped back to attention. "You don't have a brain."

A small fire ignited in my gut. Not because of what he'd said but because of what he represented. I longed for my pistol so I could rescue the two underage girls and help them find safe refuge. I certainly would have tried, anyway.

"Ah, you're too young and inexperienced." Robinson said to the girl and shoved her to the side, then pulled in one of the older women and groped her chest. "This is the finest meat in all of Asia. Am I wight?"

Slurred speech. I fake-smiled. The other girls giggled, which clearly pleased Robinson. But only for a second.

"Who has my soft dink?"

He'd misspoken again. The girls shifted their eyes to each other, but I spoke up. "I can take back these extra glasses of champagne and bring you and your friends any soda you'd like." I started to head for the door.

He chuckled and snapped his fingers at one of the women. She walked across the lavish room, opened a closet, and pulled out a gold cart that carried a covered metal tray. The Top Flight catering staff apparently had already stocked this VIP room with food. She rolled the cart in front of Robinson's position, and he moved to his knees. "Ladies, you know the routine."

One woman kept a firm grip on the cart, while the next one giggled and pulled the top off the metal tray. A second later, Robinson face-planted into a mound of cocaine.

Robinson snorted and licked and pawed at the white powder like a wild animal. He told one of the women to join him, and she did, though she seemed reluctant. I tried to get the attention of the two young girls. The one in pink caught my gaze, and I motioned with my head for her to leave with me out the door. She stood up, and I was certain I had her. One small victory at a time.

"Mr. Robinson, what have you got yourself into now?" Shek had just walked around the privacy screen, sounding a bit like a father who'd caught his son coming home after his curfew. His eyes stayed on Robinson.

The big man responded by tossing the white powder in the air. "Whee! It's raining, it's pouring, the old man is snorting. Get it? Let's all have some fun!"

I shifted my body a few inches toward the door, then tapped my ring repeatedly. I turned my torso another ninety degrees and fired off some more shots.

"She won't be very happy to see how you've messed up again, sir." Shek motioned for the ladies to move the cart away from Robinson. One attempted to do so, but Robinson still had the wherewithal to pull the cart back.

"Who wants a mother hen looking over him, Shek? I'm a grown-ass man. And a very rich man."

Shek rolled his eyes. "You know she won't approve. And you told me how much you hate when she mocks you for your, uh, extracurricular activity."

"Screw she."

He was making no sense.

Shek wiped a hand down his face. His eyes landed on me just

when another man emerged from behind the privacy screen. Spike jabbed a finger at me. "You're not supposed to be in here."

"Ah, yes. Quite right. Very well, then. I'm off. Let us know if you need anything." I couldn't get out of that room fast enough. On my way up to the third floor, I peered through the glass stairs. Spike had not followed me.

I stopped short when I reached the third floor. Two men holding assault weapons stood at either end of the expansive landing. High-pitched laughter in the distance. I smiled, gulped, and kept walking. I was being watched but not stopped. The evening was getting weirder by the second.

Su was not at the bar. I did a three-sixty—she was nowhere to be found—and then approached the bartender.

"Can you tell me where your bar mate is?"

"They took her."

My pulse skipped a beat. "Took her? Where?"

Another waiter called for the bartender, who began to head in that direction.

"Hey, I asked you where she went."

He only shrugged.

I set my tray on the bar and walked expeditiously around the third floor. No sign of Su anywhere. I went all the way to the first floor. No Su, but I did get hounded for more champagne. Back up to the second floor.

"Dammit, where are you, Su?"

"Are you looking for my dad?"

I turned to see Shek's daughter sipping what looked like whiskey.

She tapped her heels together. "Uh, I can see your googly eyes. It's not alcohol. Just a Coke without any ice. Dad would ground me for a month if he saw me drinking booze."

Booze was the least of my worries right now. "Glad to hear it."

I scanned the area one last time before moving toward the staircase.

"Hey, I thought we were becoming friends and maybe you'd ask me out," the girl said.

My mind went straight to my daughter. I flipped back around and said, "I'm probably twice your age. You shouldn't even be at this party."

"Why not? It's a great place to meet guys."

"I haven't seen any guys your age here. Most of the men are a bunch of perverts. You need to go home and never come to one of these parties again."

Her big, brown eyes narrowed.

I wasn't backing down. "Do you get what I'm saying?"

A hard metal object poked my back. I turned halfway around to have a look.

A semi-automatic rifle was pointed right at me.

31

Penha Hill, Macau

A truck motored by, and its tires sprayed water into my face.

"It is not Jet. And I don't see our catering boss or the guard with the Uzi." Su walked alongside me on the road just above Robinson's estate.

I wiped my face with my shirtsleeve and continued walking down the road. The Macau Tower lights were now shrouded in a deep fog. "An Uzi. Is that what it was?"

She nodded. "Lucky they only fired us. We were told not to engage the guests. Yet you did. Shek's daughter, of all people. Not a wise choice."

"Says the woman who went out to the van for more supplies, making me think she'd been abducted."

"Is that your way of saying you really care about me, Jack?" She covered her mouth and snickered.

I just shook my head and moved on. "Robinson is a major

league cokehead."

Another car whipped by. Not Jet.

"Not surprised, given what our Top Flight boss told me."

"Like?"

"How Robinson is so out of it mentally he can't seem to make a decision about food or drink or really much of anything."

"But he can swan-dive into a mound of coke."

"You saw that?"

I explained the entire disturbing scene behind closed doors, including how Robinson interacted with the underage girls. "I thought one of them was going to leave with me just before Shek walked in."

"Then we really would have had an incident. And you wouldn't have gotten very far."

"Unless you and your posse that's probably hiding in the shadows popped out with guns blazing."

"My posse? You are so American."

"That's funny. I was born in Salisbury, England."

She rolled her eyes.

We continued walking past palatial estates, most of which were behind walls and wrought-iron gates with fancy logos affixed to them. Su pontificated out loud. "So, we have a combination of first- and second-hand information that Robinson is a major cokehead. And if he cannot make simple decisions like what to eat or drink, then…"

"How could he be the mastermind behind this entire Viper operation?"

She snapped her fingers. "Exactly. I just cannot envision him as capable of running his casino or any of his businesses. And certainly not a trafficking business."

"So, he's not the head of the snake."

The mist turned into a light rain. I huddled under the collar of my shirt, but Su didn't flinch. She said, "True, but he is in bed with the snake. I have no doubt."

A long pause.

I asked, "Then who's the snake?"

"I'm thinking Shek."

Not a stretch. "Makes sense to me."

"We need evidence that he is running the whole operation."

"And we need to find where they're keeping the underage girls. I can't let this go on much longer, Su. It's got to stop."

She took hold of my hand. "Jack, this is personal for you. I can feel it in my bones. Tell me what is really going on."

A horn honked, and Jet pulled to a stop next to us. "Sorry I'm late."

We slipped into the Spada's back seat, and Jet hit the gas. He handed both of us towels. When I finished wiping my face, Su was staring right at me.

"So, did you guys get the goods on Robinson?" Jet asked.

"He may not be our guy," I said, averting Su's gaze.

"What? How's that?"

Su didn't chime in, so I gave him an abbreviated version of what we'd learned and observed.

"What's next, then?" he asked.

I scratched my chin and watched more estates flash by the window. "When's the last time you checked the position of that crate?"

"Ten minutes ago. Still in building three at the jockey club."

"I want to go back and check it out tomorrow."

"Given what happened there just last night," Su interjected, "how do you propose we do that?"

"That's where you come in. Use your connections and come up with something effective that will get me in there but keep me out of jail."

32

Ritz-Carlton Hotel
Cotai

Just before Jet pulled the Honda to a stop in front of the Ritz-Carlton, Su told me to give her twelve hours to figure out how to get us safely—legally—onto the premises of the jockey club.

"Not good enough."

"But, Jack, these types of things take time. I am not even sure this is possible. And if I blow my cover, nothing will work."

I shook my head, my eyes on fire. "I don't care about your cover. You either help me or I go in their solo."

She mumbled something in Cantonese, then she nodded. "Four hours tops."

"Thanks."

I exited the car and held the door open for Su, but she shook her head. "I want to find Ubaldo. For peace of mind."

"Let me know when you do."

Once I reached my floor, I yawned three times between the elevator and my room. A cool shower, and then I'd try to get in a few hours of solid sleep. From there, Su and I would figure a way into the jockey club. Get access to building three and find evidence against Shek and Robinson. The first domino to start a chain reaction that would topple the crime ring and lead me to Cai Chen.

And reunite with my family.

I reached for the door handle…and froze. When I left the room earlier, I'd affixed a small piece of tape from the door to the door jamb. One end was now pulled away from the frame. I didn't like surprises. Su's unannounced entries into my room hadn't settled well with me. Would she break in when I wasn't there? I couldn't be sure, but I certainly wanted to know. Hence, the setup with the door handle.

My pulse thrummed the side of my neck as I listened for sounds on the other side of my door. Silence.

I waited a few more seconds, peered up and down the hallway. Perhaps I was being overly paranoid. Perhaps a maid had come in.

I puffed out my chest and flung the door open. Marched inside, spun around, checked the bathroom, closet, nooks, and crannies.

Not a soul.

I sat on the edge of the bed, shoulders slumped. Though my newfound paranoia was understandable, it was changing me. My outlook on life, my temperament, even my sense of humor. I was a different man.

So be it.

My phone buzzed. Another message from Simon. I held my breath until I opened the text. Another picture of Anna and Maddie. If a heart can break and soar at the same time, mine did. They were still alive—I blew out a breath. Maddie was clinging to her stuffed animal, Woofies; Anna with one hand on our daughter. But Maddie's smile was gone. In fact, their expressions were blank. Nothing. Robotic. Almost lifeless.

I grabbed a pillow and threw it across the room. The ornate lamp flew off the side table, smashing against the floor.

I went into the bathroom and threw water on my face, looked in the mirror. Anna and Maddie were turning into zombies. The abduction and subsequent treatment were too much for them. They were slipping away.

I paced the room. *Thinking, thinking, thinking.* But all my brain could do was spit out images of my girls, the good times and then these pictures—reminders of my failures to keep them safe.

Break it down, Jack. Don't look at the whole picture. Focus on what your next move should be. One key move that will lead to others, eventually setting the entire operation on its head.

I forced my thoughts back to the task at hand, but not to constrain my thoughts.

My directive was to rescue one girl, Cai Chen. It seemed unattainable. And that was something I couldn't accept.

"Think outside the box," I said, pacing almost as fast as my brain was churning.

I snapped my fingers at the same moment a new idea shot to the front of my mind.

Abduct Shek Jian.

We could take him to a quiet location, threaten him with severe injury or even death until he spilled all the details. Names, methods, all the who-what-hows about the girls, the drugs, the distribution of both.

"Just cut the head off the snake, Jack."

It sounded easy. Maybe it could be.

My mind continued to crank. What did Simon want with Cai Chen, anyway? Was Cai a relative?

For now, it didn't matter. Cut the head off the snake, rescue the girl, and my girls come home.

I seethed. The lump in my throat was replaced by bile teasing the back of my tongue. I envisioned what I might do if I ever had the chance to confront Simon, whether that was a person or group. I let my imagination run wild for a few minutes, until I realized I was clawing my forearm. Angry, red tracks of blood. Matching my thoughts.

I pulled my hand away. I couldn't do this to myself. To Anna and Maddie. They would need me, healthy in flesh and mind.

It was time to convince Su. On my phone I pulled up her contact and…

The door flew open with a resounding *whap*. Uniformed men—the Macau police. I jumped to my feet, but they grabbed my arms and held me in place. Voices filled the room, words I didn't understand due to language barriers, as more officers rumbled inside.

Must have figured out I was the interloper at the jockey club. "What do you want? You can't be in here. It's my room."

One man with gray at his temples barked orders in Portuguese. Officers fanned out and started searching the room.

"What do you want? Maybe I can help you."

I knew my protests were pointless. This was China. I had no rights. No one did.

I was ignored by everyone. I had no idea what they were looking for, but whatever it was, they wouldn't find it in here. Other than a change of clothes and toiletries, I had nothing.

A high-pitched voice, and all heads turned toward the far wall. The safe was open, and an officer held up a baggie.

"What is that?"

The lead man with the graying hair took the baggie from the officer and dangled it in front of my face. It looked like crack cocaine.

"That's not mine. I have no idea where that came from. I'm just here on business."

He smiled until he showed yellow, cracked teeth. "You are under arrest. Take him away."

33

Judiciary Police Station
Taipa

For the third time since I'd been locked up, I turned my back to the annoying man in the cell next to me. Speaking in English, he was putting a lot of effort into trying to make me think this swing through the Macau judicial system would not end well for me.

"You know what happens to pretty blond boys in our prison, right?" He laughed and howled, and others joined in.

My platinum hair. I'd almost forgotten. I curled my hands into fists. So many changes in the last ten days. And now I was a jailbird, still not one iota closer to saving my wife and daughter.

I took the stupid manual I'd been given on the way in and smacked it off the iron bars.

"Awww, pretty boy is upset. Does he want to go home to his mommy?"

I pinched the corners of my eyes, tried to maintain calm

breaths, hoping I'd wake up from this nightmare and everything would be back to normal. With Anna and Maddie and our beautiful lives together.

Two guards walked into the holding area. I wondered if they'd confirmed my innocence, that the drugs weren't mine.

The first guard stopped at my cell and started to insert a key, but the other one barked out an order in Portuguese. The first guard rolled his eyes and shifted one cell over. He opened the door, cuffed my laughing nemesis, and the three of them walked out of the holding area.

The nauseating chatter and mocking laughter had ended.

I released a sigh and considered how long I'd be in this cell before I'd be told the charges against me, interviewed, allowed to see a lawyer…something. As much as I tried to live in the moment and not envision the worst, doubt had already started to creep into my mind. Doubt that I'd be able to convince anyone that the drugs were planted in my room. Doubt that I'd be able to walk out of this jail a free man any time in the next few months or even years. Doubt that I'd ever see my wife and daughter again.

I spun around and threw the manual against the back wall. "Dammit!"

A rage that had boiled inside for days had to come out. I needed to inflict pain on someone. The people who'd stolen Anna and Maddie. But my enemy—the true enemy—was completely unknown to me. I had no idea who or what Simon was. Or where they were located, where they were holding my girls. If I had even a clue, I'd unleash some serious kind of hell on anyone in my path.

I dropped to the floor and leaned my back against the wall. My fingers felt the paper edges of that damn manual I'd been given by a man with a round face and round body, a patch on his yellow shirt. The patch had *Human Rights Organization* written on it in three languages.

I picked up the booklet and began to read in earnest. Lots of block paragraphs in tiny print. Some pages had been ripped out. On other pages, some lines of text were covered in black marker. Redacted. That got my attention more than the surrounding words.

My eyes landed on one particular sentence where it stated the police had to ensure a person in custody would go before a judge within forty-eight hours of detention.

Forty-eight hours. An eternity.

I came upon the section that spoke about the length of time prosecutors had to either charge or dismiss a detainee. Six months. Damn. And I'd thought forty-eight hours was a long time. I flipped through a few more pages, then focused on the section that included a reference to the People's Republic of China.

My brain whirred on three key phrases. *Final interpreter. Not subject to appeal. The Standing Committee.* This was what I'd feared. The real truth of living in an autocratic state. They gave you the impression they cared about human rights, but this Standing Committee had the authority to move in any direction they saw fit.

A harsh reality set in. I was a Westerner using a fake identity. Working with an MSS agent—though I wondered if that was a good thing or a bad thing. That made me leap to the question I should have asked myself hours ago: who set me up? If I could figure out *who*, that might give me some idea on how I could get out of this mess.

I ran through every person I'd encountered, including Su and Jet. While there was potential incentive for each person if I was arrested and thrown in jail for months or years, sadly, I couldn't eliminate any of them. Not even one.

Keys rattled, and the door to my cell opened and a familiar

face appeared. “Mr. Fishbeck.” It was the officer who’d led the raid in my hotel room, the one with the graying hair. He instructed his much younger cohort to enter and cuff my wrists. Then he popped his knuckles and said, “It is time for your interrogation.”

34

The interrogation room was just as barren as my cell, aside from a framed sign that adorned the white wall: NO SMOKING, in three different languages.

A man in a blue suit and red tie blew out three puffs of smoke, each in the shape of an oval. Ironic that a man in a position of power was outwardly rebelling against the sign's directive. Likely that was precisely the point. Rules were for everyone else.

When he snuffed out his cigarette on the floor, the officer who'd brought me into the room quickly scooped up the remnants and threw them in the trash. If there was any question about who had the higher rank, it was just answered.

The man in the suit opened a manila folder on the desk in front of me, picked up one sheet of paper, and held it at eye level. I couldn't make out any specific words but did notice none of it was in English. "Mr. Clayton Fishbeck," he said, addressing me for the first time.

I wasn't sure where he was going with that, using my fake name. But it gave me hope that my identity ruse was still in play.

He then told me his title. No name, just his title. I must have blinked ten times while he rattled off the alphabet soup.

"I can see you're lost. Just call me Shŏuxí."

"Shŏuxí," I repeated.

"It means Chief."

I almost asked him, "Chief of what?" but it didn't matter. My fate clearly rested in his hands. Those three phases from the Human Rights manual flashed before my eyes: *Final interpreter. Not subject to appeal. The Standing Committee.*

"Now, Mr. Fishbeck, before I begin to ask you a series of questions, I think you need to know a couple of facts." He paced back and forth a few times, then leaned on the table and eyeballed me. "We notified the UK embassy of your arrest and confiscation of your passport."

On the surface, that was good news. They were buying my fake identity. Of course, that happy balloon could be popped in a hot second when UK officials revealed I was unknown to them, didn't exist, was a fraud. The British would undoubtedly turn their backs and not give me another thought, and I'd be left without any support system. The term "rotting in jail" nibbled at the back of my skull.

"Thank you, Chief," I said, hoping he'd appreciate the show of respect.

"The charges against you, while not yet formally presented in a court of law, will fall under two main areas of concern: drug possession and drug trafficking."

Drug possession *and* drug trafficking?

After a quick glance at the officer—he was staring me down from under the brim of his hat—I rotated my head back to Chief.

"You must have a couple of cases mixed up," I said. "Your assistant over here and his squad raided my room and found a baggie of something. I had never seen it before. But before we address that sham, I'd like to make sure we're on the same page. The drug trafficking charge is completely bogus."

"Bogus," he said with a friendly bow of his head.

While nodding, I was distracted by the officer scrunching his shoulders, as if bracing for a flash-bang.

I saw the blur of Chief's hand only a split second before it smacked the table. The force behind it was so great that his tie blew over his shoulder. "I gave you facts, Mr. Fishbeck." His spittle sprayed across my face. "Do not insult me by telling me how to do my job. Is that understood?"

"Yes." I clasped my hands until my knuckles turned white.

"Now, as I was saying…" He brought his tie to the front and centered it on his button-down shirt. "These charges hold a minimum term of fifteen years imprisonment."

He continued talking, but none of it registered.

Fifteen years…

My heart and soul had fallen through a trap door as I tried to digest the idea of spending any time in a prison, much less fifteen years in a foreign prison. Away from my wife and daughter. Would Simon hold Anna and Maddie that long? If I was unable to complete the mission, what would be their fate? Bile crept up my throat.

"Now that you understand my role and how this will work, do you have any questions about the process?"

He had to be mad. I had a million questions, and I understood nothing. But I said, "Not right now."

"Very well." He removed a pen from his front pocket and pulled a piece of paper from the manila folder and set both in front of me. Then he tapped the paper twice. "You can start by writing down all the contacts in your network. If you are fully cooperative—and that will be determined by me—then special accommodations could be considered for your sentence. But I must emphasize, you cannot give us the runaround. You must be specific and thorough in your cooperation."

I shifted my sights from the paper up to Chief. He picked up the pen and handed it to me.

"You want me to do this now?"

He nodded. "I don't believe in wasting time, Mr. Fishbeck. Start with giving us these contacts and all other details about your drug trafficking operation, and then we can talk further."

"My drug trafficking operation. You seriously think I'm the person running this?"

He turned his head slightly and cocked an eyebrow. His eyes were cold, unfriendly, agitated. "We have strong intelligence indicating this is true. Are you saying you report to someone else?"

I set the pen down and rubbed my temples before speaking. "I don't report to anyone, because I have no affiliation with any drug trafficking operation. Furthermore, I don't do drugs of any kind. That baggie was planted in my room. Not sure who did it, maybe someone from your own police force, but it's not mine."

Chief whirled around and pointed at the officer. "Is it so, Captain Danilo…that you or someone on your force planted drugs in Mr. Fishbeck's room?"

Danilo shrugged. "I have been in this role for seventeen years. These foreigners come in here and throw their money around, soil our culture at every opportunity. I do not have to plant anything. They do it all on their own. Why? Because they think they are better than anyone."

I sensed a small window of opportunity had opened. Time to flip the dynamic. "I'm sure your job is extremely difficult, Captain. I can't imagine how you deal with so many people who act like they're privileged. Maybe we can work together to figure out who put the drugs in my room."

In reality, I wanted no part of working with law enforcement on anything. The person who'd planted the crack in my room undoubtedly knew things about me that I had no intention of sharing with the police. They might even figure out I was the person who'd been running around the jockey club. My words were nothing more than a Hail Mary.

Captain Danilo smirked. "You are a desperate man, Mr. Fishbeck. I have seen many people in that same chair try to lie their way out of their predicament. But your manipulation skills are rather impressive."

"That crack is not mine. And I'm not a leader of any drug ring. It's not lying if I have no clue about it."

Chief stuffed a hand in his pocket and walked across the room. He paused, then walked back, each step deliberate.

"This is the end of our first interrogation session, Mr. Fishbeck. Twenty-four hours from now, we will have our second. At that time, if you refuse to offer your assistance, then we will assume you are a foreign enemy of the state. And I will be forced to take additional measures to retrieve the information I need."

I was promptly escorted back to my cell. When the door locked behind me, Captain Danilo started to snicker. "Chief has a variety of ways to retrieve information, especially from those who wish to take advantage of our people. You should be prepared to share everything you know or you will suffer the consequences. Simple as that. Pleasant dreams, Mr. Fishbeck."

35

I tried to swallow, but there was no moisture and I coughed. Chief whirled around and stared me down for the umpteenth time in the last three hours—my second interrogation event.

Rings of sweat on his shirt armpits were now almost meeting in the middle of his shirt. His tie was completely undone, draped around his neck. He'd gone through about a dozen cigarettes, and smoke hovered at the ceiling as though time had frozen. The room smelled like a locker room. But my stomach was queasy for another reason. Neither Chief nor Danilo, who was positioned by the door, had believed anything I'd said. And after Chief had made a phone call, they'd both gone quiet.

"I hope you know that I'm not trying to disrespect you or your country," I said, hoping to re-age them, to ultimately appeal to their humanity.

Chief glanced at me, then spoke in Portuguese to Danilo, who looked into the hallway. They were waiting for someone. And that someone was likely some type of amputation specialist.

Hopefully just a staged threat.

A man in a cheap suit marched into the room holding a black medical bag. He spoke quietly to Chief, nodded as if acknowledging the order, then came over to the table. He began to remove instruments from his bag and set them on the table. Sharp instruments. My body broke into a sweat.

"What's going on?" I asked.

I searched the eyes of Chief and Danilo. They wouldn't look at me. Then I addressed the man with the medical bag. "Do you know English?"

"He will not answer your questions," Chief said. "He has orders to carry out. That is all."

"What orders?"

No response.

My mind tried to plot how I could escape the room. But two seconds later, three large, uniformed men entered, spoke to Danilo, then walked to my chair, and held me in place. "What are you doing?" I grunted, struggling to move.

Chief walked over and put a finger in my face. "You are holding out on us. This I know deep in my gut."

"I've told you everything I know. You don't want me to make it up, right?"

He backed up two steps, and the doctor moved next to me, brandishing a large scalpel.

"Come on, let's talk this out."

Chief shifted his eyes to the ceiling.

"Do you fucking hear me?"

He ignored me. They all did.

The next sound was me screaming until my voice cracked.

***

I tasted sweat at the edge of my lips. At least it wasn't blood.

Almost twenty-four hours later, and from the floor of my cell, I turned my bandaged hand over and stared at the end of my left ring finger. It was now shorter, thanks to the doctor's handiwork.

My tortured finger throbbed relentlessly, the rhythm resonating up my entire arm. The doctor had given me an antibiotic to stave off infection after he'd cleaned up the wound. Part of me wanted to ask how a doctor, someone who'd taken an oath to heal the sick and wounded, could purposely harm another person. The answer probably fell in one of two categories: extortion or a big payoff.

I pulled from my pocket a small baggie that contained five pills—painkillers. Oxycodone. Courtesy of a fellow inmate, whose lawyer had smuggled them in for him. The inmate, who was just taken out of his cell, had taken pity on me and given up his stash. I stared at the pills like they were individual neutron bombs covered in sweet chocolate. Enticing me. Threatening me. Pills had nearly ruined my life back in college, and I'd vowed to never again take another prescription painkiller. I would never have a reason to do so.

Until now.

Even after a night of no sleep, I was wired. Actually, it felt like I'd been tasered directly in my spinal cord. A bird landed on a perch just beyond the tiny window of my cell. Bobbed his head, looking at me. Perhaps he was frustrated because he could see no way in. I was losing hope there was any way out.

Take the pills, Jack. Make your troubles disappear. The pain in your hand, the hole in your heart. Poof—it all goes away.

Soon, the cell door would open, and once again, I'd be escorted into the same interrogation room. Same shit, different day. My third session. Chief warned me that lack of cooperation this time would cost me an entire finger. This would continue each day until I ran out of fingers, and then they would start on my toes. Then arms and legs. Somewhere along the way, I would get smart and confess. Chief's logic.

I paced, then stopped and stared at the pills again, wondering how much longer I could hold on to my sanity.

The pills are your ticket to paradise, Jack. Just take them and say goodbye to everything out of your control. You deserve some peace.

I closed my fist and shoved my hand back in my pocket. My thoughts bounced between a scalpel severing my finger to wondering what my girls were feeling at this precise moment. Their fears. Their pain.

More pacing, my shirt drenched in sweat as the internal debate reached a fever pitch.

The familiar jangle of keys echoed.

My delay game had saved me from a likely overdose. But there was a tradeoff. I'd have to watch the good doctor remove an appendage. What would presumably be the first of many.

36

Chief loosened his tie and rolled up his sleeves. He'd been verbally lashing out at me for at least an hour. I was frustrated about being asked the same questions repeatedly. My responses hadn't changed. Not yet. I was still battling inwardly about what I could share with Chief that would bring me freedom and not sabotage my mission. But it was *his* frustration that mattered most.

"I can wear a wire," I blurted.

Chief and Danilo stopped what they were doing and looked right at me.

"A wire." Chief waltzed closer to my chair. "That implies that you do have information, and thus far, you've decided not to share it."

"Look, I'm just an entrepreneur who's looking for the next big thing. But I'm pretty good at schmoozing."

"What is this schmoozing?" Danilo asked.

"Kissing ass. Sucking up to people so you can get something

you want."

They both nodded as though well-versed in the concept.

"Just point me in the right direction, and I'll go wear a wire so you guys can capture everything that is said."

Chief cocked his head and looked off toward the corner of the room as if his curiosity had been piqued. After what seemed like an eternity, he turned his beady eyes back to me. "I see through your bullshit, Mr. Fishbeck. You know who the players are. And you have sixty seconds to start writing them down on that piece of paper." He started a timer on his watch, sat on the edge of the table, and glared at me, nostrils flaring.

My internal clock started counting the seconds. My pulse moved at twice that pace. After several beats, I noticed the pen in my right hand—I'd unknowingly picked it up. What the hell was I going to write down that would save me and preserve my ability to complete my mission?

Nothing, that's what.

My handcuffs clanged against the table as I set the pen down. "I want to speak with someone from your MSS."

Chief's eyes shot lasers at me. Danilo eyes didn't blink. My eyes bounced between the two, wondering if one or both would come unglued and start pummeling me.

A rhythmic beep sounded from Chief's watch. The deadline had arrived. Without taking his eyes off me, Chief tapped a button on his watch, and silence returned.

Not for long.

Sirens wailed, and a light on the ceiling flashed red. Chief shouted something at Danilo, who shrugged. He had no idea. They shouted at each other, the siren preventing them from having a conversation at a normal volume. Danilo rushed out the door. People raced along the hallway. Seconds later, Danilo ran back into the room and stood mere inches from Chief's face, shouting. Chief shouted back. If only I were a lip reader…and was fluent in Portuguese.

Chief threw his arms up, then let them smack against his thighs. He was pissed at someone, or maybe just the alarm. Something he couldn't control. He whipped around and jabbed a finger in my direction as he approached the table. He was about to lose it on me.

But he stopped like he'd run into a wall. He hurried to pull his phone from his pocket and eyed the screen. Then he covered one ear and shifted to the corner of the room. I looked at Danilo, who was wiping sweat from his forehead. He seemed antsy. Through the crack in the partially open door, I saw more people rushing by, some in handcuffs.

There had to be a fire, and a potent one if they were moving prisoners to another location.

Chief pocketed his phone and spoke into Danilo's ear. Chief wasn't animated. If anything, he seemed strangely calm while relaying the message. When he left the room, another officer, Danilo's sidekick, rushed into the room, and the pair came over to my chair and pulled me upright.

"Where are you taking me?"

Neither said a word. They guided me into the hallway and down three flights of stairs. People were everywhere, stressed looks on many faces. But I didn't see any smoke or fire. On the first floor, we followed a large pack of officers and their prisoners down a corridor that eventually spilled into a garage. Prisoners were being escorted onto three buses.

My mind instantly started to run through possible escape scenarios once I was on the bus. There had to be power in numbers. First step, I'd need to convince a few other prisoners—the nastiest I could find—that we needed to rebel and overpower the guards.

I veered toward the first bus.

"No." Danilo pulled me back, and we bypassed all three

buses.

"What?" My eyes scanned the garage for another prisoner bus. There were only cars and people rushing around. Thick, gray smoke billowed from behind a vent in the far garage wall. I now understood their urgency.

"Shouldn't I get on that bus back there?"

The two officers ignored me and marched up an incline that led to the second floor of the garage.

"Guys, I think we need to—" I didn't see the end of the club until I was falling to the ground, air rushing from my lungs. Danilo's temples all bluish, bulging veins. His cohort next to him, glaring down at me.

"You will not say another word," Danilo said through gritted teeth, "or I swear you will not be alive by the time we reach our destination."

37

On the road out of Macau

I didn't say another word. Instead, I focused on breathing—a wet, raspy sound.

Danilo's sidekick pulled me up, and we walked at a brisk clip until we reached a plain white van. Danilo opened the back door, shoved me inside, and slammed the door shut. No seats in the back, just the metal shell. A moment later, with Sidekick driving and Danilo in the passenger seat, the van pulled in behind the prisoner bus at the garage exit.

The bus turned right. We turned left. And my level of concern doubled.

We were in the heart of Macau's central district, on Avenida de Amizade. Friendship Avenue, from my limited understanding of Portuguese. Up on my knees, I could see through the front windshield. The road forked, and we veered to the left. Towering buildings, a billboard for the Sands Casino, another one for the

Grand Prix Museum. We passed them all.

Sidekick continued on Friendship Avenue, which carved a path in between two bodies of water. Some type of reservoir on one side; a larger bay that fed into the ocean on the other. A ferry terminal made me think of Tom from the Full Moon Marina and how I'd pretended to need a boat to woo a girl, all to get closer to Shek. Another lifetime ago.

We rimmed the north side of the city, where a thick fog hovered above the taller buildings.

Soon the city was behind us, and we were crossing a bridge over water. We'd just left Macau. A few smaller buildings hemmed the side of the land in front of us, but it was the tree-filled mountain that stood out.

Danilo pointed to it while speaking in rapid-fire Portuguese. I only picked up one word: caverna. Had to mean "cavern." I wasn't thrilled about the implications.

On a two-lane road, Sidekick made his way to the bottom of the south side of the mountain. Not even two kilometers into this leg of the trip, Danilo barked out an order, and Sidekick slammed on the brakes. He shifted the gear to reverse and turned a sharp right onto a dirt road that was barely wide enough for the van. Wiry branches smacked and scraped the sides.

Moving at a brisk speed, the van rolled through countless potholes, and my body bounced off the metal floor. The bruises would eventually heal, if I lasted that long. I could almost predict my final moments. They'd push me out of the van in some remote location and put a bullet in my head. Wildlife would feast. Ashes to ashes, dust to dust.

We rounded a bend in the road, then traversed more potholes during a sharp decline. When the road leveled out, the van's speed slowed. Danilo turned and glared at me with eyes that had only one message: I would soon die.

But I wouldn't go easily.

I spotted a set of keys on Danilo's belt. I knew he wouldn't hand them over voluntarily.

Turning away from the front, I stuck my finger down my throat and instantly started to wretch. I pretended to fall on my side, vomiting. I could hear Danilo and his partner yelling at each other. I began to convulse, grunting and groaning loudly. I sounded possessed. Danilo got out of his seat and moved closer to me.

I rammed my head straight into his nose. He shot back, screaming as blood streamed. When he slammed into the back of the van, I jumped for his keys. A mad scramble, slapping, clawing, wrestling…

One of his hands accidentally hit the latch on the back doors and they flew open. The van was still moving. He punched me in the jaw, then grabbed me by the cuffs and dragged me toward the front. I pulled away and fell on my back—my legs were now in play. When he leaned over to reestablish control, I clocked him in the head with my left foot. He staggered, and I dove for the keys, grabbed them with both hands. His belt loop snapped. He then went for his gun. I took hold of his arm, we struggled, and the gun went off. A scream. His partner had been hit. The van swerved violently left and right, slinging me out of the van. I hit the ground with a hard thud before rolling two, three, four times. I spit out dirt just as the van crashed into a tree.

Steam hissed through the front hood, but there was no human movement or cries for help.

I was battered and bruised, but I was free.

38

Xiangzhou, Zhuhai
Guangdong Province

"Come on, come on." Now on my fourth key from Danilo's key chain, none had fit my handcuffs. I gave it another few seconds, then moved on to the next key.

Five was my lucky number—Maddie's age.

I unlocked my handcuffs and tossed them into the woods. As I hiked back to the main road, I knew I'd have to find someone with a phone and make a call. I didn't know who had set me up, but with no other options, I'd likely have to test the waters with Su and Jet.

It took me about fifteen minutes to make it to the two-lane road. From there, I walked down a short hill toward a row of small homes nestled near the water.

No one answered at the first house. On the second, an elderly man wearing reading glasses answered the door and gave me a stern once-over. Said I looked like I'd been on the losing end of a brutal fight. I didn't elaborate. He agreed to let me use his phone, but only if he could listen in.

Su answered on the second ring, and I gave her a brief description of where I was. Oddly, she didn't ask me any questions about where I'd been the last three days. "Jet and I will be there shortly. Do not bring attention to yourself." And then she hung up.

I thanked the man and waited outside for no more than thirty minutes before Jet drove up in his Honda Spada. I practically fell into the car. Once he punched the gas, I let gravity pull my head back against the seat, and I closed my eyes.

"Jack, your hand," Su said. "What happened?"

I opened my eyes. Found myself questioning Su's motive for partnering with me. The entire experience was bizarre. I considered the idea of a broader conspiracy in play, where she and Jet had planted the drugs in my room so they, through the police, could see if I knew more about the Viper operation than I'd let on.

With my good hand, I rubbed the back of my stiff neck.

"Jack, you are not talking. What is going on?"

"I've been through hell the last three days." I waved my bandaged hand in front of her nose. The end of the nub was soaked in crimson. She jerked her head back. I said, "I'm wondering if I can trust anyone."

"You think we planted that crack cocaine in your room?"

I shot up in my seat. "How do you know that drugs were planted in my room? How do you know about any of this?"

She reached over and touched my arm. I pulled away, and she said, "We have contacts at the hotel. One of the bellmen told me everything. That is when Jet and I started to brainstorm on how to get you out."

I took a moment to test her words and body language for

authenticity. I gave her a passing grade. "Continue," I said.

"Jack, with you being an expat, plus using a secret identity, it was almost a certainty the police would use their most intimidating methods to pull information from you." She looked at my hand. "You are hurt, and you need help."

I explained the torture method used by Chief.

"I am so sorry you had to experience that. I am ashamed to be associated with the leaders of China for imposing such horrific punishment."

"Thanks for saying that." I glanced out the window. We were crossing the bridge back to the Macau peninsula.

"Jet is driving us to his apartment in the northwest corner of the city. He lives in a small place above a coffeehouse."

"I know a doctor who can treat your wound," he said.

"Thank you." I turned to face Su. "Now, can you explain what the hell happened back at the police station?"

"I set the fire in five dumpsters just behind the station."

"You knew they'd take me offsite?"

"That was our goal. We thought you would go with the other prisoners and just hoped you would have a chance to escape."

I explained the van ride, the fight for the keys, and the crash that allowed me to escape.

"Holy fuck," Jet muttered.

"I'm just glad it worked. I was looking at months if not years in prison." I blew out a slow breath. "We need to talk about our next steps."

"First, we must tend to your wound and get you some food. Whatever our next step is, you will need to be sharp, both mentally and physically." She paused a second. "Unless you are done with this whole thing. Are you?"

"I'm in this until the end. So I can go back home."

Su gently touched my arm. "To Tennessee, right? How long have you worked for the CIA?"

I shook my head. "Look, you can call me Jack, but that doesn't mean I'm an open book. You only need to know that exposing and stopping these despicable human traffickers is as personal for me as it is for you. It's the only thing that matters in my life. End of conversation."

39

Jet's apartment
Macau

I awoke to the sound of Jet's voice. He was speaking quietly in the adjoining room. Still drowsy thanks to a sleeping pill Su had given me, I propped myself up on my elbows so I could hear the conversation more clearly.

I shifted my feet beneath the covers, inadvertently knocking a box of gauze pads to the floor. The other room went silent for a moment, then, "Jack, you up?"

Su poked her head in and waved. I grunted and wiggled this way and that until I was sitting up against the headboard.

"How long was I asleep?" I asked, wiping my sticky eyes.

"Just over two hours. How is your hand doing?"

I studied the bandage work Jet's friend had done on my finger. A pre-med student who attended Macau University of Science and Technology. While she redressed my wound, she'd reminded me at least three times that MUST was the first university established after the handover of Macau to the People's Republic of China.

"Good enough," I replied.

"For what?"

"For whatever's needed. Let me get some water, and then we'll talk about our next move." I flipped my legs over the edge of the bed and pushed up to a standing position, only to lose my balance and drop back to the bed.

"I will bring the water to you."

A minute later, with Su in a chair next to the bed and Jet leaning against the doorframe, I finished off the full glass of water.

"Another?" Jet asked.

"Not necessary." I turned to Su. "Hey, did you ever speak with Ubaldo?"

"Briefly, over the phone. He is practically working nonstop right now."

"On what?"

"He could not share much because he was being watched, but it sounded like he is doing legwork for the drugs that Y2K is peddling. That is exhibit number one as to why we need to blow up this whole operation."

"He'll be okay. He's a survivor."

Su nodded and let her hands drop to her thighs. "Okay, I have—"

"I need to share an idea with you." I cleared my throat to get their full attention and said, "I want to kidnap Shek."

I counted to ten, waiting for a response. Jet's saucer eyes shifted to Su, but neither said a word.

"If I offended some Macanese tradition with my idea, I don't really care. We know Shek is bad news. We know he's in the middle of all this. Which means he has information. I figured let's go right for the head of the snake. Or who we believe is the head of the snake. What do you think?"

More silence.

"No responses? Seriously?"

"I am thinking, Jack." Su started to kick her leg.

"That's a frickin' suicide mission, Mr. Whitfield." Jet's voice pitched higher now, the intensity turned up a few notches. "I mean, if we can pull this off, we'll all have to leave this place and start a new life under a new identity. Or be killed. No joke." He ran a finger across his neck in a slicing motion.

I turned toward Su. "But if we get all the dirt from Shek, solid evidence of his role and everyone else associated with Viper, then there won't be anyone left to retaliate. Am I wrong? It just seems logical to me."

Jet looked at the floor, pursing his lips while Su just sat there, stone-faced and kicking her leg.

"Tell me the MSS hasn't done this type of thing before," I pressed. "Hell, the CIA has done that and more."

Seconds ticked by. I was not a patient man, not anymore. But I waited.

Su blew out a breath and lifted from the chair. "Before you were arrested, you wanted us to figure out a way to inspect the crate at the jockey club."

"Yes, I did. I do."

She turned to Jet. "Does the tracking device still show the crate at the club?"

Jet held up a finger, then pulled out his phone and tapped the screen a few times. "Yep. Building three."

"Even after three days, huh?" I said. "Maybe it's not as important as I'd thought, or hoped."

"Or maybe Shek or Spike or that mystery person you saw that night at the jockey club removed the contents," Jet said.

I shrugged. "It's possible. Either way, crates don't talk.

People do. And if we can get Shek to talk, then we'll save a shit ton of time. We might end up saving lives. Just think about all the girls being sold as sex slaves."

Su started nodding slowly, as if she'd just been convinced.

I pointed at her. "You're on board."

She was on board, finally. "Okay, now we can talk logistics," I said.

Su took center stage. "Normally, we would take a good couple of weeks to map out every place Shek goes and then find the perfect location to snatch him. During those two weeks, we would also find a vehicle that has never been used, the right equipment, weapons, and a location in which to interrogate him."

"Su, we don't have two weeks."

"I know. So, as much as this pains me, we will need to condense that down to three days."

"One day," I countered. "I'll need a gun, first off. We'll find out where he lives and follow him around. When we see our opportunity, we jump him, throw him in the back of Jet's Spada, and head to the hideout. And I know the perfect place."

Jet tilted his head. "You do?"

"Personal experience, right, Su?"

She ignored my comment. "Three days."

"One."

"Three."

"This is supposed to be the quicker option, right?"

"Quick and full of risk."

"Okay, can we meet in the middle?" I pleaded.

"Two days. No less."

Two days was the time frame I'd really wanted the whole time. The art of negotiation. At least one skill from my old life had been put to use.

40

Taipa East

Hidden in an alleyway in the cover of night, I waited behind the wheel of a moving van, my foot tapping the floorboard. My nervous energy could power the entire city of Macau.

Two days of data. That was all we had to go on in terms of Shek's routine. At my accounting firm, if anyone had suggested making an important financial decision based upon such a small sample size, we would have laughed.

But the decision to kidnap Shek and coerce him into spilling the details about Viper was solely based on the urgency to save lives. The lives of my wife and daughter. And all the girls who were being sold like livestock. The odds were not in our favor, but we had to try. There was too much on the line. Failure was not an option.

I touched the earbud Su had given me, which allowed us to communicate on a secure line. "Do you see him?" I asked.

"Not yet. Five minutes out." Su was positioned up the road from our "trap" zone.

Shek had left his thirtieth-floor apartment at The Manhattan at the same time the last two evenings. His destination each time was the main bar at Studio City, the same hotel where Su and I had watched him have a drink five nights prior. From there, Shek would then move to the blackjack tables in the casino. After winning a substantial amount, he then hit three other casinos, finally finishing his gambling binge at Wynn Palace. Just before dawn, he would head back to his apartment until the next evening. During the day, he never left his apartment, as best we could determine.

While we openly wondered if Shek would follow the same routine on a third straight night, one data point tonight gave us hope. Su had received info from a contact inside the apartment building. Shek would be in a silver McLaren Speedtail, driving alone. No Spike. No bodyguard of any kind. No companion. But that didn't mean he couldn't dial up any number of thugs within seconds.

We assumed Shek had a gun in his car, but we knew he couldn't take it into a casino. We considered trying to abduct him just as he entered Studio City, but we couldn't predict how someone close by might react if they saw Su's pistol. Too many variables.

Thus, plan B was born: snatch Shek just after he left his apartment building.

My moving van was large enough to stop any vehicle from crossing Window Road, a small one-way road just south of the roundabout near Shek's apartment building. Once Su gave the signal, I would pull forward, blocking the McLaren's progress. Su would pull up behind the McLaren. When Shek got out of his car, Jet would do his thing—a skill he'd told us about earlier in the day.

"Jet, you ready?" I asked.

"Always, Mr. Whitfield." Jet was standing in the dark next to a dumpster, perfectly positioned to hit the target once we boxed him in.

"You said that before, Jet," Su chimed in. "Yet when you demonstrated your skill, you could not hit a tree from ten feet."

Jet's skill was shooting a blowgun. When he'd originally sold us on the idea, it sounded as though he was fairly proficient at it. Turned out he was closer to a novice level.

Jet laughed, but it was nervous laughter.

"Jet, you said you would practice all afternoon."

"I did, Commander. Just you wait and see. I'm a clutch performer."

I didn't share his optimism. My anxiety was off the charts, in fact. The tip of the blowgun, upon hitting its mark, would inject a sedative. Key words: *upon hitting its mark*. If that didn't happen, Shek could pull out a weapon, possibly shoot to kill. Su and I could offer a defense with our own weapons, but we didn't want to inadvertently kill the guy who had the information we sought.

"I see him."

Su's words startled me, and I squeezed the steering wheel. "Is he getting close?"

"Jack, he just pulled out of the parking garage. Give us two minutes to reach your location. Jet, you've got the blowgun loaded?"

"Yes, Commander."

"And you are confident you can hit a moving target? Shek is a small man, so you must be very accurate."

"I swapped out blowguns. I'm now using my Cold Steel Professional 625."

I jumped in. "Did you practice with it?"

"Not really. The 625 is said to be effective up to twenty yards."

"That should work."

"In fact," Jet continued, "they say a skilled shooter can hit a two-inch circle up to ten yards away."

"Turning south on Window Road," Su said. "No cars between Shek's McLaren and our Spada. Get ready for my call, Jack."

I shifted into drive but kept my foot on the brake and waited for the "go" call. My heart pounded my chest—and not just because we were about to pull off a risky abduction of a very wealthy, powerful man. It was more about finally closing in on Viper, exposing them, and rescuing Cai Chen.

All of which would take me back to Anna and Maddie. The only thing that mattered.

I pulled the baggie of oxycodone pills from my pocket, gave them a final farewell glance, and tossed them out the window.

"Now, Jack. Go!"

I punched the gas. Pulled out of the alley. Bright lights to the right of me. Shek honking his horn. I hit the brake and put the van in park. Shek stopped about ten feet from the van, Su just behind him. He had no way out.

Shek honked the horn three times. Tried to back up. Honked again. If he kept honking the horn, someone would eventually call the cops. And if I was arrested by the Macau police a second time, I might lose more than a finger. I'd bet all the money in Macau that Chief realized he'd been fooled into letting me go. If given a second chance with me, Chief would make it worth his while. My slow and painful demise.

"Su, could Shek be calling in reinforcements?" I asked.

"Maybe. Dammit. If Spike and others show up, that'll derail our plan. And we're sitting ducks. Especially Jet."

I shot a quick glance at the side mirror. Jet was invisible from his perch on the side of the road. "Jet, you still with us?"

"I'm right… Hold on. The car door just opened!" Jet said.

With the headlights still partially blinding me, I only saw Shek's silhouette, still seated, as his arm held on to the open door. I clutched my door handle, ready to jump out the moment Jet shot the blowgun. It would take mere seconds for me to reach Shek, scoop him up, and drop him in the back seat of the Spada. *And away we go.*

I stared at the McLaren. No further movement. Shek's hand seemed to linger on the door for too long.

"I don't like this. He's taking forever to get out of the car," I said.

"It is not easy getting out," Su said. "Those luxury sports cars are so low to the ground."

"Sounds like you've been in a few."

She didn't reply.

Shek finally emerged from the car.

My gut hit the floor.

The dark figure was tall, wide.

Not Shek.

"It's Spike!" Su said.

"The bigger they are, the harder they fall," Jet said.

I heard a muted *thunk.*

"I hit him, I hit him!"

Spike's upper torso jerked all around. He lifted his huge mitt of a hand and swatted at his arm. How long would it take for the sedative to work on a guy that big? "He's trying to pull the dart out!" I yelled.

I heard some rustling through my earbud, then Jet yelled, "He's coming right for me!"

I jumped out of the van.

41

Spike growled as he lifted Jet by the neck and shook him. No second-guessing this. I bolted out of my stance and ran right at the Neanderthal.

"Hey!" I leaped into the air, feet first. Spike turned his head. The sound of my shoe hitting his chin—like breaking walnuts. I slammed to the ground on my hip. Spike wobbled but stayed upright. He did, however, loosen his grip on Jet, who pulled away, coughing and gasping for air.

By the time I moved to my knees, Spike had shaken off his cobwebs enough to grab my foot. He glared at me with crazy eyes. "You can't hide behind that platinum hair. You're gonna wish you were dead."

He twisted my foot counterclockwise, which would have snapped my ankle if I hadn't anticipated his move. I followed the motion with my body, then flipped myself over the leg he was holding. I clipped his nose with my shoe. He shrieked and let me go.

Rapid footfalls coming closer. Su, with her gun drawn.

She said, "Stop moving. Down on the ground."

Of course, Spike did not comply.

Just as Su skidded to a stop, temporarily losing her balance, Jet jumped on Spike's back and started to claw out his eyes. Spike surged forward in spastic fits. A wayward fist from Spike smacked Su's gun, which skittered out of sight.

"Get the gun!" I said to her. "I'll get Spike."

She ran off and slid to the ground, searching in the darkness for her pistol.

Jet was still tugging at Spike's eyes. Spike continued to flail, but he couldn't shake the kid. Only one way to take down a tree—chop it at the trunk. I rammed my foot, full force, into Spike's knee. It bent unnaturally, and Spike began to topple over.

Jet fell off his back.

"Grab your blowgun! Put another dart in him!" I yelled.

Jet snatched up the blowgun, aimed, and let it rip. The dart stuck in the back of Spike's thigh, and he dropped all the way to the ground. I ran over and blocked Spike's hand from pulling out the dart.

"Leave him."

I turned to see Su standing over us, a phone in one hand, her pistol in the other.

"What's up?"

"Just got a call from my source at The Manhattan. Shek took off in a black Mercedes. Let's roll."

"What about Spike?"

Jet lifted Spike's arm; it limply dropped to the ground. "Down for the count."

Perfect.

42

Su left rubber on the road as she backed the Spada away from Spike and the idle McLaren. She whipped the wheel hard to the left, and the front end did a one-eighty. Then she punched the gas.

"Hot damn, Commander!" Jet hooted. "Hey, what about the van?"

"It's a rental under a fake name," she said. "They'll never tie it to me."

I scanned the road for a black Mercedes. Only saw two motorbikes. Actually, three…four…

Like rabbits in Donelson.

White-knuckling the steering wheel, Su was laser-focused on catching up to Shek. We quickly reached a road with more traffic. "Which way?" I asked.

She hooked a right on Noble Oak. "Source said he was heading south."

As she gained speed, we blew by homes nestled in an area of

trees, then shot under the crossing to the Taipa Elevator. There was a monstrous building just around the bend.

"Grand Royalton apartments," Jet said from the back.

I turned to Jet. "You think Shek could be meeting someone there?"

"It's possible," Su said before Jet could reply. "Keep your eyes out for that damn car."

A ramp veered off the main road toward the front of the Grand Royalton. Both Jet and I scanned the ramp and drop-off zone for a black Mercedes. "You see anything?" I asked.

"No, dammit." He huffed out a breath and pounded his fist into the palm of his other hand. "Once Shek finds out we ambushed his muscle, he'll know we were really after him, right? Then he'll probably add a bunch of extra security. Hell, he might hire some type of black-ops assassins to figure out who did it and come after us."

"I think you've been watching too many Bourne movies."

"Do not dismiss what Jet is suggesting," Su said. "People with money in China can sometimes have a cozy relationship with members of law enforcement so they will turn a blind eye at the right time."

"Bribes."

She nodded. "I have heard of instances where the ultra-wealthy have a security force that is not just used for protection. They take a more offensive approach, if you get my meaning."

"Black ops, man. I'm telling ya," Jet said.

I noodled on that idea for as we entered a roundabout and, beyond that, a sea of colorful lights. "The Cotai Strip is just ahead."

Su tapped a finger to her chin. "Shek could be starting his normal nightly routine. Studio City is at the end of the strip."

"He took a different car, though. You think he knew we were tracking him?"

She tilted her head from side to side. "Possible, but switching up at least a part of his routine occasionally could be normal protocol." She paused, narrowed her eyes at me. "Something we would have learned if we had allowed ourselves adequate time to surveil him for at least a couple of weeks."

I retorted with, "We didn't have that kind of time."

End of subject.

Traffic increased. Mostly cars and motorbikes were moving at an average speed. "Can you weave in and out of the traffic, go faster?"

"You want to get pulled over by the police? We will be delayed, and your mug shot has probably been distributed to every officer in Macau."

I didn't like her answer, but she was probably right.

"Black Mercedes!" Jet smacked my seat.

"Where, where?" I whipped my head to look in every direction.

Jet said, "The parking lot to the left. Macau University."

Su turned us around in a flash and headed toward the university parking lot. Just as we pulled into the lot, Shek walked inside the building—the engineering school. We found a spot in the back row.

"What's he doing at the university?" Su pondered, tapping her chin.

"Probably visiting his daughter," I said. "When I met her at the Robinson party, I pegged her for a teenager, so she could be in college."

"Should we snatch him once he walks out of the building?" Jet held up his blowgun. "I've still got two darts."

Su and I glanced at each other for a few beats, then nodded. "We will have to wing it," she said. "Jet, you can hide in the bushes next to the steps. Once he is out, shoot him with a dart. Jack will pretend to tie his shoes. Once Shek starts to drop, Jack will grab him like he is just drunk or something. I will drive up, and Jack will toss him inside. And then we are off. Sound feasible?"

"Too late," I said, pointing to the front door. Shek walked down the stone steps, then got into his car and drove out of the parking lot. "We need a new plan." Cursing, I pounded the dash.

43

Wynn Palace
Cotai

Shek didn't speed or make any evasive moves in his Mercedes. "Wonder where he's going now," I said.

"Hopefully some place isolated so we can kidnap him." Jet pounded his fist into the back of the seat.

"He's turning into Wynn Palace," Su said.

Water was on both sides of the road, but our eyes were fixed on the spectacular fountain show taking place before us. Music blaring, lights blazing. The luxury resort reminded me of videos I'd seen of the Bellagio in Las Vegas.

Su pulled into a parking lot as Shek continued to the magnificent porte cochere.

I started to open my door, but Su grabbed my forearm—and it wasn't gentle. "You cannot go in there, Jack."

"But we need eyes on him. He might be meeting someone we

want to know about."

"With that hair, he'll remember you."

Jet raised his hand. "I'll go."

"You can't get caught," I said.

"You need to take pictures and stay out of sight," Su said, adding, "And you can't get caught."

He gave us a thumbs-up. "Can't get caught. Got it. Back in a flash."

He zipped away, either unafraid of the potential danger or blind to it.

"I like his enthusiasm, but I worry about his inexperience," Su said as we watched Jet walk inside the hotel.

If she only knew that I was the least experienced of our small team. By a mile. "Jet has some rough edges, but I just think it's because he's young."

I could feel her eyes on me. Without turning in her direction, I said, "Why are you staring at me?"

"I'm still trying to figure you out."

"There's really not much to figure out. I'm pretty simple."

"I am perplexed. A strange feeling for me."

"Perplexed about what?"

"You, Jack Whitfield, a.k.a Clayton Fishbeck. You act like you are not affiliated with American intelligence agencies. And there are times when I actually believe that to be true." She strummed her fingers on the steering wheel. "You are an enigma, Jack. That is exactly what you are."

"You're not exactly an open book yourself."

"I have shared more with you than anyone in the field, MSS or otherwise. What about you?"

"I'm only focused on this one mission. Blow up this Viper operation and save the girls. That's it."

She nodded. "There is more to it. I feel it. Maybe you will tell me. Or maybe I will find out another way."

"Focus."

"On what?"

I pointed straight ahead. "Jet's running this way."

She faced the front. "Why is he running? Doesn't he understand the art of subtlety?"

Jet jumped inside the vehicle, panting like he'd run a mile.

"What is so urgent?" Su asked him.

He held up a finger. "Two things. First, Shek's paying off a boxer."

"You saw money exchange hands?" I asked.

Su followed with, "How do you know the man was a boxer?"

Jet looked at me. "Shek handed him a thick envelope. The guy opened it and thumbed a few bills." He turned to Su. "I asked a bellman, who told me the guy had just lost a bout against the former Southeast Asian champ."

"The same fighter we saw the other night. Shek is fixing fights," I said. "Might be using it to launder his excess cash from Viper."

Su asked Jet, "What is the second thing?"

"I wanted to hurry and get to the car before Shek walked outside, and I didn't have time to make a pit stop."

Su's shrugged, palms up. She wasn't following him like I was.

Jet bounced in his seat. "Seriously. You got a bottle I can pee into?"

Shek's Mercedes drove right past us. I said, "Let's go."

44

Full Moon Marina
Coloane

After we tracked Shek in his black Mercedes to the Full Moon Marina, Su, Jet, and I huddled on the roof of the Spada in the abandoned parking lot next to the marina. From our vantage point, there were too many boats to see individual people. "Is that…?" I shifted around to get a better view. "I think I see Shek walking near the—"

"Let me see!" Jet jumped up, and his spastic movement bumped me off the roof. I hit the ground on a knee and rolled onto my shoulder. Fortunately, I managed to protect my bandaged hand in the process.

"Jack, are you okay?" Su asked, poking her head over the edge of the roof.

"Uh…" I got up, rotated my arm at the shoulder socket. "Nothing that won't heal, I suppose." As Su chided Jet for his clumsiness, a tiny, piercing light swept across my vision.

I walked closer to the origin of the light, somewhere through the thick row of hedges that bordered the marina. I shoved a few prickly limbs aside, reaching a metal fence, and looked again. At this angle, I could pick up a somewhat unobstructed view of the docks in the southwestern section of the marina. Two marina employees were loading crates into a large speed ferry. Once they finished and walked off, Shek came into view. He stepped onto the boat, holding the rope that had been tied to the dock cleat, and started the engine.

I backed out of the hedge and shared my intel.

"He must have had this little trip planned before he left his apartment," Su said.

"Right. I'm going after him."

"Jack, you cannot."

"I can. And I will. You won't stop me, Su." I started marching toward the road, intent on entering the marina and renting a boat.

"You have no idea where he is going."

I paused.

She continued. "It will take some time to rent a boat. You cannot just run up, whistle down a cab, and then tell them to follow that boat. On top of that, Tom has already seen you, right?"

I leaned over, hands on knees, shaking my head for a few seconds, then turned around. "I'm sick of doing nothing."

"Nothing?"

"Okay, well, we just aren't making progress fast enough."

"Can we see the name of the boat? Then we can try to track down the owner."

I plowed through the shrubs until I was inches away from the metal fence. The boat was just starting to pull out of the marina. Couldn't find a name on the boat, at least not where a name should have been. As it gained speed, another person came into view next to Shek. A woman.

I updated the crew, and the news seemed to energize Su.

"Ubaldo told us he believed the vultures were using unmarked speed ferries to bring the girls across the harbor from Hong Kong." Su tapped her chin as she seemed to consider this new development. "Can't say who the woman with Shek might be, though."

"Did either of you see a woman in Shek's Mercedes?" I asked.

They both shook their heads.

"Jet, did you see a woman talking with Shek at the Wynn?"

"Nothing comes to mind. But after he paid off that boxer, I ran out of there. So it's possible he met a lady, and she went along with him."

"Or she could have been in his car from the beginning, at his apartment," I added.

"What are you getting at?" Su asked.

"I can't nail it down. Not yet."

No one spoke for a few moments as our mental gears spun.

I broke the silence. "The silhouette figure at the jockey club. That was a woman. We need to go back. I want to look in that crate."

"I still need to figure out how to get us in there first," Su said.

"Do it quickly. I don't want to wait until daylight."

Su started pacing. I did the same. Jet, meanwhile, started jumping up and down.

Su scowled at him. "What is wrong with you?"

"I need to—"

"You are like a little kid. Go in the bushes." She rolled her eyes, then said to me, "I have a plan. But you will need to wear a onesie."

45

Macau Jockey Club
Taipa

Su got us into the jockey club before daybreak, but only by a few minutes. An orange glow lit up the eastern sky just enough for me to move around without running into another employee.

I'd originally feared entering the club with other people on site, but I shouldn't have worried. Dozens of club employees and jockeys were all busy preparing for a day of racing. Wearing an official blue onesie and matching cap allowed me the anonymity I sorely needed. Hiding in plain sight.

While I shoveled manure, Su, in her black leggings and practice riding gear, was speaking with one of the club's maintenance managers.

"When you are done in that stall, hit the stable on the other side of the track," a crew leader barked at me before moving on.

Cap low, I continued to shovel, one eye on Su. I had

confidence she'd convince the manager to give her the keys to building three—without him even knowing he was being manipulated.

Someone in the locker room called out for the manager, and he started to step away from Su.

"Shit," I said under my breath.

A second later, he turned back around and tossed a set of keys to her. She strode past me, winking. "Looking good in your onesie, Jack."

She walked toward building three as I shuffled over to my next manure pile. My eyes were on her as I shoveled. When she opened the door and stepped inside the building, I scooted in that direction, scanning the area as I went. Coast clear. I set my shovel down and entered the building. Smooth as ice…

For all of three steps. I froze, shocked. There had to have been a hundred crates in the one-story building, some stacked to the ceiling. "Ho-ly…"

"It is a little overwhelming," Su said. "And they all look the same."

I removed my cap and scratched my head. "No way we have enough time to check all of these to find the one with Jet's tracking device attached to it."

Su ran her hand along the sides of the crate directly in front of her. "I agree. Too many. We may need to come back tonight."

"How would we get back inside the building?"

"I might have to charm that manager more than I care to."

"You'd sleep with him?"

"I have done worse."

The admission made me cringe, but every option was on the table to locate the trafficked girls and rescue Cai Chen.

"Let's try to make some headway," I said, gesturing toward the crates.

Su started on one side of the room, and I on the other. After each crate, we'd glance at each other and shake our heads. Our own operational process. One crate after another, none had the tracking device. After my first ten, I decided to open one just to make sure I wasn't missing anything noteworthy. It was filled with horse-racing magazines. I asked Su to check the contents of a crate on her side.

"Just a bunch of files, receipts, invoices, whatever." She checked another crate. "Same in this one. How about you?"

I pulled the lid off a nearby crate. "Just old clothes. Strange." The word of the week. As I snapped the lid shut, I picked up a whining sound. I paused and turned toward the door.

"You hear something?" Su asked.

"I think it's the mower outside." I ran my hands along the side of the next crate. Nothing. After two more stacks, I decided to change my approach. I wound my way through the crates until I reached the back wall and restarted the search.

"Jack, if the crate with the tracking device was recently put in this room, it would be closer to the front."

I poked my head around a ten-foot stack. "But what if they didn't want it to be found? They might put it way in the back."

Silence.

"You agree with my logic, don't you?"

"Okay, you are right on this one."

I reached up and felt along the crate on the top. Nothing. With six more crates under this one, I didn't want to waste time pulling each one down. I walked around the tower of crates to conduct my tracking-device inspection on each one without unstacking them. The wall was in my way, so I grabbed the bottom one and pulled the stack. It only moved an inch. I grunted as I pulled again. No joy.

"Must be lead in these crates."

"Need some help?"

I peered around the corner and came face to face with Su.

"Girl power?"

"I am all woman."

"Right. How could I forget?"

We both grabbed the bottom crate, leaned backward, and pulled. It moved about a foot. A quick breath. We adjusted our grips. "We'll do it this time," I said. "On the count of three. One, two—"

"Wait." She stood up straight and turned her head.

"What?"

"I heard something."

"The mower? Is someone coming?"

She turned back to the crates and lowered her head. I followed her gaze to the floor. A small triangular section of wood built into the floor protruded from under a crate. We locked eyes for a second and, without speaking, grabbed the bottom crate and pulled like maniacs. On our third heave, we finally cleared the crates from the suspicious section of the floor. I dropped to my knees and knocked on the wood.

Nothing.

"Maybe it was just the mower," Su said.

I knocked on the wood again and lowered my ear to the floor.

Two faint knocks replied.

I shot up. "Someone is in there!"

There was no obvious handle, so I felt around the edges of the wood, looking for a release button or something to pull. Su dropped down beside me and…another sound. We both got squirrel still.

A whimpering noise.

"A girl's voice," Su hissed, and we frantically searched for a way to open the trap door.

My fingers ran across a slight bump at the end of the last plank. Pressed the bump, and the door popped up about three inches. I yanked it all the way open. Su pointed her phone's flashlight into the hole.

Two girls. One down on her side, moaning. The other, with matted hair, reached up. "Help us?"

I offered my hand. "Yes, we will help you."

46

With two bottled waters tucked into my coveralls, I glanced over my shoulder toward the track. The riding mower had been shut off, and more people were starting to enter the club grounds on the far side. For the moment, no one was looking in this direction. I slid inside building three and hustled to the back of the room where Su knelt next to the two girls sitting on crates.

"Here you go," I said, handing a bottled water to each girl.

The girl who'd spoken to us earlier cracked the top of the bottle, pulled tangled strands of hair from her face—her long hair dropped all the way to her lower back—and chugged. The second girl, who had a deep cut under her eye, didn't have the same energy. When she struggled to remove the cap, I did it for her and handed her the open bottle. Her hand quivered from the weight, so she used two hands to bring it to her lips. Water spilled down the sides of her mouth, but she continued drinking.

"How long have they been in there?" I asked Su.

"They say they do not know for sure."

“Who put them in there?”

She gestured with her hand to slow down a bit. “We can ask them questions later. They are understandably frightened and malnourished. We—”

“Is this the work of Shek?”

“I saw tattoos on their ankles. Some kind of snake.”

Air rushed from my lungs. “They were branded, like Ubaldo said he’d heard.”

She nodded. “They need care.”

“Okay, how do we get them out of here? We can’t just escort them out the front gate.”

“I would guess most club employees do not know about this hidden room. If they do, they probably would be horrified to learn that girls are being held down there,” she said.

“Most, but not *all* employees. We really have no idea who’s part of this horrific act. Which is why I want to ask the girls a few questions.”

She arched an eyebrow. "Just around the corner from the front door of this building is a ten-foot wall that separates the club grounds from the alley. That will be our escape route with the girls.”

“I can try to lift them up to the top of the wall, but you’ll have to—” I stopped cold. I’d just heard an explosion in the distance. “What was that?”

“Start a two-minute timer.”

“Was that Jet?”

She nodded. “He created a diversion in the concession stand behind the grandstand.”

“He’s blowing the place up?”

“He is making them think it is a terrorist attack. In reality, he only mixed a couple of volatile ingredients in a gallon container. He also set a bunch of paper products on fire.”

“Damn good idea.”

"Thanks for your approval. Help me get the girls over to the door."

She ushered the girl with the long hair, while I held out my arm to allow the weaker girl to use it as a crutch. Her footing was uncertain.

"You're doing great." I wasn't sure she understood me, but I gave her a reassuring look. She attempted a smile, but there was too much pain on her face for it to shine through.

Once at the door, Su's phone dinged. "Jet is bringing a ladder to the other side of the wall in the alley."

"I didn't see a ladder in the Spada."

"He is in the limo now, and he borrowed a ladder. Do not worry about it. We need to be quick outside the door until we are around the corner and the side of the building is shielding us from the east side of the complex."

I stepped out first. A small plume of gray smoke corkscrewed above the grandstand on the north side of the track by the concession area. I waved at Su to follow, then I picked up the second girl and carried her around the corner. A second later, a ladder appeared just over the top of the wall.

"You there, Jet?"

"Yep. All clear on this side."

Su nodded—we were also clear on our side. "Jack, you get to the top of the wall, and I will push the girls up to you. Then you can guide them down the ladder. Jet can help with the last few rungs."

I took two running steps, planted a foot against the wall, and launched myself upward. I twisted my torso at the last second and landed on the top, facing the infield. I gave Jet a thumbs-up, then straddled the wall and lowered my arms toward Su. "Ready."

Su explained the plan to the girls in Cantonese, and then she lifted the stronger one until I had a grip on her forearms. I pulled while she used her feet to crawl up the wall. Her agility and strength surprised me. Once safely next to me, she took a breath, and then I helped her down the first few rungs of the ladder. "You got her, Jet?" I kept my hand around her arm until she reached the last rung.

"We're good," he said.

One down, one to go.

People yelled in the distance, and I looked up. Two men were running across the infield in our direction, waving their arms.

"We've got company. We need to pick up the pace here."

Su tried to lift the other girl off the ground, but it was like lifting jelly. She had practically no strength. The two men were now crossing the near-side dirt track. The proverbial sand was starting to empty from the hourglass.

I anchored my body by grabbing the side of the wall, then lowered my torso toward Su. "Just give me one of her arms."

Su brought her closer, and the girl took my hand. I said, "Your arm. Let me grab your arm."

Su did a quick interpretation, and the girl let me take hold of her upper arm.

"Got her?" Su asked.

"Yep." Pulling with all my might. More shouting. I looked up. The men were now running through the grass track. I recognized one of the scowling men as the crew leader from earlier.

The girl slipped from my grip. She cried out, but I caught her before she fell.

"You sure you got her?" Su asked, flipping around to look toward the infield.

"Yep." But I wasn't sure. The girl had sweaty arms and the strength of a toddler. I could now hear the men's shoes whipping through the grass—their shouts also closing in—but I kept my focus on the girl. "Come on, you can do it."

She began to speak in Cantonese. I couldn't understand her, but the pained expression on her face told me everything. She was giving up; she completely let go.

I caught her by the wrist—a miracle.

I started pulling her upward, but it was as if she were working against me. She was slipping out of my grip one more time. "Su…" I grunted as sweat poured off my face.

Without me saying another word, Su pushed as I pulled. The girl drew closer, but only a few inches at a time.

I heard one of the charging men yell, "They are stealing she's cargo. Stop them!"

His English interpretation wasn't perfect, but I clearly understood their position: *enemy*.

We only had seconds. But if I squeezed the girl's arm any harder, I could break a bone. "A little more, Su. Come on!"

The girl surged upward a good foot. From there, I was able to use both of my hands to bring her to the top of the wall. She nearly fell over the side from sheer exhaustion. We didn't have time for her to catch her breath. "Ladder," I said, guiding her legs to the first rung. "Need your help, Jet!"

"All over it."

The girl took hold of the ladder and stepped down one rung. Shaky. I had a grip on one of her wrists. Jet had her covered from below. I swung my sights over to the club side. Su was about ten feet back from the wall now. The men were nearly on top of her. One with a lead pipe, the other with a hammer.

"Here I come." She raced to the wall, planted a foot about four feet up, and bounced upward. I was still holding the girl on the ladder, so I had only one arm to offer Su. She took it and torqued her body in some crazy way, landing on her feet on the top of the wall. A real-life Spider-Woman.

"Holy shit, Commander!" Jet said from the other side,

The man with the lead pipe smacked the wall just under my

foot. A second later, the crew leader hurled the hammer at Su. She ducked and jumped to the ground next to Jet. I was right behind her. We grabbed the girls and ran as best we could, given their weakened state.

"What about the ladder?" Jet said while running backward.

"We're alive," I said. "If we want to stay that way, get us to the limo and drive like a bat out of hell."

47

Jet's apartment
Macau

Su poked her head into the bedroom at Jet's apartment to check on the girls, then walked past me into the small kitchen.

"So…?" I prompted.

"Jet's medical friend, Angelique, is still tending to Liang."

"The one with the cut under her eye."

"Yes. The other girl, Huan, has washed off and is resting. Angelique will give us a full report when she is done tending to Liang's cut."

The front door burst open. My heart nearly shot out of my chest. I dropped into an athletic position and grabbed the first thing I could find. A coffee table book: *The Secrets of San Francisco*.

"Sorry if I scared you, Mr. Whitfield." Jet smiled and shut the door with his foot.

I growled and set the book down.

"Anyone follow you?" Su asked, taking one of the bags of groceries from Jet.

"Nope, not as far as I could see."

"Which is it—no or only as far as you could see?" I asked.

Jet turned to Su as if wanting her to rescue him. She only shrugged and said, "I was going to ask the same question."

"I did just as you said. I went down to the cemetery and the park, walked around that area for a while. No one followed me. I went to the market, bought these groceries, and then quickly backtracked to see if anyone was following me or watching my place. We're all clear."

Su made up some plates of egg rolls and fruit for the girls. Jet delivered the food, then minutes later, he returned with Angelique by his side.

"How are they doing? Can they talk yet?" I asked the pre-med student.

Angelique removed nitrile gloves, threw them in the trash can, and washed her hands. "They're both malnourished and dehydrated. You saved them, I think, just in time to avoid irreparable damage to their major organs. I wish they were in a hospital so they could be monitored."

Su and I locked eyes, and Jet stepped in. "Hey, Angelique, do you think you can check in on them every few hours?"

I added, "We'll pay you."

"I can get you the first payment by tomorrow," Su offered. "Will that be okay?"

Angelique nodded, but her eyes were darting around the room. Clearly, she wasn't comfortable operating in this type of setting.

We stood in an awkward circle, a quiet one. "We have all sorts of food here, Angelique," Jet said.

She grabbed an egg roll from the counter and took a bite. She seemed to relax some.

"When do you think they'll have the energy to speak to us?" I asked.

"Hard to say," she said. "Once they eat, they might sleep until tomorrow. By the way, they both showed me bruises all over their bodies. They were abused pretty badly. The younger one, Liang, started to tear up as she talked about it. Even with their poor health, their mental wounds might take far longer to recover from."

The treacherous balancing act: get information without traumatizing the girls in the process.

Jet shared his frustration on the subject out loud. "Dammit. First, we lose Shek, and now that we have a real chance to learn all the dirt, we have to wait." He popped a wedge of pineapple in his mouth and chewed aggressively.

"I can talk to you," a girl's voice said.

It was Huan, standing in the doorway.

"Are you sure you don't need to sleep?" Angelique asked.

She shook her head.

"Was the food acceptable?" Jet asked.

"Very good. Thank you."

Su motioned for Huan to take a seat on the couch, and she did. Angelique left, saying she'd be back to check on the girls in a couple of hours. Jet verified that Liang had fallen asleep in the bedroom.

"You speak good English," I said.

Huan nodded. "Thank you for saving us."

"I'm sorry you were in that room." I really had no idea how to approach the questioning. The last thing we needed was for me to make her upset. Not good for her, not good for us. Thankfully, Su stepped up to the plate.

She sat beside me on the ottoman and clasped her hands. "If any of these questions are too tough to answer, just let us know.

We are only asking so we can find the people who are responsible for this and—"

"Chain them up like animals in the hull of a ship? Keep food and water from them? Beat them, rape them?" She brought a shaky hand to her face and thumbed a tear.

Su reached out to the girl, stopping just shy of touching her. "Huan, I am so sorry," she whispered.

Huan sniffled. "Do not be sorry. I just…I want them to suffer."

"They will. I promise you that," Su said.

"Tell us about this ship you mentioned."

Huan inhaled a deep, shuddering breath and released it. "Mogwai."

"Monster," Jet muttered.

"Is that what it means?" I asked.

"Yes." Huan straightened her back, even though her bottom lip was quivering. "Most of the bruises on my body, Mogwai gave to me. Same with Liang." She lifted her chin toward the bedroom. "I will have a lot of nightmares from Mogwai."

"How many other girls were on this ship?" I asked.

"In our area, I think forty or so when we started out."

"What about when you landed?"

"Mogwai killed at least three girls that I saw. Maybe more. It was—" She stopped, and it was clear she was holding back a sob.

Jet offered Huan some water. She accepted, downed most of the bottle, and wiped her mouth. Then she shared the stories. How Mogwai killed the girls with his bare hands, and the crew knew it. How no one tried to stop him. On and on. When she finished, she was staring at the floor, the three of us in hushed silence.

After several long seconds, Su picked up the questioning. "You said you weren't sure how long you were in that underground room. Do you know who put you there? Names, anything?"

"It was a little crazy. But Sly was the one in charge."

Su and I shared a glance, recalling the unusual name. Sly had been one of the two men with Shek at Full Moon Marina.

"Do you know why you were being held in that underground room?" I asked.

"We were to be sold to someone very wealthy and powerful men in Macau. But Liang and I were actually lucky."

"Why do you say that? You suffered greatly," I said.

"There was another girl with us. But they took her."

I shifted to the edge of the ottoman. "What other girl? Who?"

A cough from behind us. We all turned to see Liang wiping her eyes, a hand on the doorframe. "Cai. But she dead." Liang began to weep.

48

My pulse couldn't race any faster. Yet I wasn't moving.

With two feet anchored shoulder-width apart, my hands crossing my chest, I stood in front of the lone window in Jet's living room, watching the masses down below go about their lives. I didn't see any one person. I was focused instead on the pictures in my mind. The pictures I'd received of Anna and Maddie in captivity. Their stress. Their fear. Their strength. Then I envisioned the unsavory faces of those involved in this twisted enterprise: Sly, the Y2K Triad leader Liou Changming, Robinson, Spike, and the faceless monster, Mogwai. But Shek was at the top of the list. The man was vile.

Jet was off to switch the limo for the Spada. Angelique had returned and was now in the bedroom with Su, checking the girls' vitals. Just before she'd arrived, Huan clarified what Liang had told us about the third girl in their underground room.

Cai.

"When they pulled her from the room, Cai was crying a lot,

and Mogwai started smacking her around. It did not look good. But we really do not know for sure what happened to her."

I still had hope.

Su walked out of the bedroom. "Jack, we need to talk."

"I'm right here," I said but continued to stare out the window. She approached and gently turned me to face her.

"I can see the intensity in your face," she said. "This other girl, Cai…do you know her?"

I shook my head, turned back to the window.

"Jack, please do not play these denial games with me. We may not have time."

"That's the truth. I've never met her."

"But you know *of* her." She paused, tapping her chin. "She has something to do with your mission."

I couldn't hold out any longer. Not if I expected Su's help to find Cai—if she was still alive. "Yes," I said, now looking her straight in the eye. "Okay? You happy?"

Unfazed, she said, "I could ask you twenty more questions, but I do not want to waste my time. We can save that for later."

"Good. Just know that I have to find Cai. Alive."

"I understand. I am just not sure where to start."

"We need to review every piece of evidence, every interaction we've had with Shek and the sicko bunch of them."

She nodded and pressed her hands against her face as though she were praying. Eyes wide, she rocked from side to side.

"Let's start with Sly," I said. "Huan mentioned him, and we know he was one of the guys talking to Shek at the marina. I think if we find him, then we might find Cai."

"If he still has her. He might have already turned her over to the buyer."

"We need to start the trail somewhere, Su. And we beat the shit out of anyone until they give us the information we need. And the next one, and the next. Ultimately, we'll find the person who has her."

"What if they do not want to be found? What if they are so rich, they pay people to lie for them?"

I heard my breath hiss through my teeth. "The power of my fist will win that battle."

"Jack, this is more than a mission to you. Tell me."

Feeling my emotions bubbling to the surface, I ignored her comment. "Who else besides Sly?"

Jet rushed into the apartment and threw his keys on a table. "All good," he said before joining us at the window. Su caught him up to speed, then pulled out her phone and seemed to be checking for messages.

"Something important?" Jet asked.

"Just Ubaldo. He is ignoring me again. We must blow up this whole Viper operation, so Ubaldo, Wen, and all the girls will finally be free."

Su began to pace, so I turned to Jet. "You sure no one followed you to the apartment?"

He snapped to attention like a good soldier and said, "One hundred percent!"

Angelique opened the door and asked us to keep it down.

When the door closed again, Jet winced and said in a low voice, "Sorry. But if you hear my phone going off, it's my taxi company boss flapping her gums, trying to get me to pick up some big party at Wynn Palace. I don't jump just because she talks. Screw her."

Something he'd just said tickled my subconscious thoughts. What had piqued my interest? I couldn't nail it down. A memory, something I'd seen or heard…

"That's right." Jet continued the diatribe about his boss. "If she orders me to do anything, that'll be the final straw, man. Jet will no longer answer to her."

"You mean, she?"

"Huh? Are you making fun of my English? It should be pretty damn good considering it's my first language, Mr. Whitfield," he said with a chuckle.

"I'm just remembering a few conversations…" We walked into the kitchen where Su was cleaning up the countertop. "Something doesn't quite fit right. Maybe you two can help me."

"I will try, of course," Su said.

I let it rip. "Shek, at Robinson's party, said the following: '*She* won't be very happy to see how you've messed up again, sir.' A few seconds later, he told Robinson, 'I just know *she* won't approve.'"

Su grabbed my arm. "Does this mean Robinson is answering to a woman?"

"Hold that question." I peeled Su's grip from my forearm. "Robinson answered Shek by saying, 'Screw *she*.'"

"Must have misspoken. He meant 'her,'" Jet said.

"He was coked out of his mind," I admitted. "But still, it was strange."

"English is Robinson's first language," Su said.

That was obvious—he was a Brit—but he could have stumbled over his words because of the excessive drug use. Yet, I wondered…

"Let me add one more data point to the equation. Back at the club, when Su and I were struggling to get Liang up to the top of the wall, the men who were running for us—"

"Damn, I still can't believe the commander did that Spider-Woman move. Whoa, it was killer cool." Jet grabbed an apple, tossed it in the air, then took a bite. Grinning the whole time.

Su shook her head. "Go on, Jack."

"The men were screaming at us. Most of it I couldn't understand. But I heard the crew leader say one thing that stuck out: 'They're stealing *she's* cargo.' Now, while I think the crew leader's first language is either Portuguese or Cantonese, he spoke pretty clear English when talking to me. Pretty sure he wasn't coked up either."

"Mr. Whitfield, I just don't get these word games. In fact, it's kinda making my head hurt." The smirk was gone, and Jet was scrunching his shoulders, grabbing his head. He turned to Su with a pained expression. "Am I just dense, or are you feeling the same thing, Commander?"

She didn't respond. Her hands were against her chin in the praying position, her expression blank. Jet snapped his fingers in front of her face. "You with us?"

"Unless you want me to break those fingers in five places, I would not do that again."

"Yes, Commander." He dropped his hand and took two steps back.

I said, "Based on what I saw from Robinson, it's hard to believe he could lead any organization. We've already discussed that. We thought Shek had assumed control—or had been in control all along. I still think he's very involved, but now it seems like a woman very well might be the head of the snake. What do you guys think?"

No verbal responses. A head-nod from Jet. Su acted like she hadn't heard a word I said. I sure as hell wasn't going to snap my fingers at her, so I waited her out. During the silence of the next thirty seconds, the only notable sound came from the bedroom. Laughter. And it warmed my heart just a little bit.

"Okay," Su finally said. "We may have stepped into a very combustible situation."

I frowned, confused. "I'm not following."

"First, I agree with your assertion that Robinson is not running the show. Maybe he was in the beginning, but not anymore. Shek has a pivotal role, but he is not the leader either. It is a woman, yes."

"You're three-for-three, Mr. Whitfield," Jet said before Su's stare made him shrink in his stance.

"In Chinese culture, women who are beautiful in appearance but crafty and ruthless in their heart are called 'beautiful snakes.' Now, snakes have a very prominent role in our culture. Lots of symbolism and many stories going back centuries. But the key thing here is that the Chinese word for snake is—"

Jet finished her thought, "Shé, with an accent over the e."

I did a slow nod. "So, it has two meanings: a woman and a snake. The organization is called Viper. Snakes all around. But who could *she* be? That's the big question. If we figure that out, we'll be on our way to rescuing so many." I looked at Su. "Cai and other girls. And we can get Ubaldo out too."

"This is where…"

"Where what?" Jet pressed.

Su closed her eyes for a brief second, then opened them and swallowed hard. "There have been rumors that a certain leader has been too closely aligned with the elite and not focused on the people she governs. I am speaking of the chief administrator of Macau, Xela Chang."

I held up a finger. "Those chants at Senado Square. I asked if you believed she was a puppet to Beijing."

"More like a puppet for the elite, the worst kind of elite. The richest people and the ones who hold no respect for China or its citizens."

My mind was nearly in spin mode as I tried to process what was being suggested. "They shouted, 'Xela is a traitor to our people.' Do you really think Xela could be shé, the head of Viper?"

A ping. Glass shattered. "The bedroom!" I bolted in that direction. Su grabbed her pistol off the counter, right behind me as I blew through the door.

Liang was on the floor, moaning, blood draining down her forehead. Huan and Angelique were huddled next to her, sobbing and shaking. I threw myself on top of the girls as Su raced to the window, gun drawn.

"See anything?" I shouted.

As the girls cried and quaked beneath me, Su aimed her gun toward another apartment building across the alley. A few tense seconds passed, then she lowered her weapon.

"He is gone."

"You saw the shooter?"

She nodded and glanced out the window one more time.

"Can you describe him?"

"Not needed. I know who it is."

I waited, held my breath.

"It is Wen. Wen tried to kill the girls."

49

Penha Hill, Macau

Cai Chen untwisted the end of a metal coat hanger, then used it to pry the edge of the vent in the locked closet of the pool house. Perspiration poured down her face like rivulets, stinging her eyes, but her intensity never wavered. It couldn't. Within minutes, Mogwai would return. He had beaten her several times—it seemed like a game to him—but before he left the last time, he'd said he just might kill her upon his return because he'd grown bored of her.

Murder by boredom.

The monster had killed at least a dozen girls on the cargo ship. Of the girls who'd survived, most had already been farmed out to their new owners. They were treated like animals. Worse than animals. Cai wondered what had happened to the two girls who had shared that space under the jockey club building. Had they been taken to their new owners? Or had they died from a lack of food and water?

Even as her heart beat wildly, Cai refused to yield to her fear. Of Mogwai. Of her potential new owner. Of all the bad people who didn't give a shit about her life, or the lives of the other girls.

She carved out a chunk of the wall and wedged her fingers behind the vent's metal lip and started to tug. Her fingers slipped twice, but then she began to make headway. Her energy doubled, and within seconds, the vent was almost completely off. She was naturally petite, and that, along with the malnourishment she'd suffered after being kidnapped in the Philippines last week, would allow her to slip through the opening. Once outside, she would find her way off this estate, and then she would disappear into the mass of people.

"Come on, just a little bit more."

The closet door opened, and she lurched. Mogwai chuckled, but the laughter didn't last long. Cai spun on her knees and drove the jagged edge of hanger into his thigh. As he bucked upward, screaming, she scooted between his legs and darted out the front door of the pool house.

She didn't run for long. She bumped straight into another man and dropped to the ground. The man with the creepy little patch of hair on his chin.

"Mogwai. Bring her to my room."

"Yes, Shek," Mogwai grunted.

Mogwai moved the bloodied hanger to within an inch of Cai's face, then threw it to the side. "This, I cannot wait to see. What Shek does to pretty girls like you is far more painful than my approach. He is methodical. And he loves his toys." He chuckled as he lifted Cai off the ground by the back of her neck. She kicked and clawed at his wrist, but it was like being tethered to a meat hook. A futile exercise.

Inside the mansion, Mogwai tossed Cai into the bedroom,

and the door shut. Her jaw opened, but no words were spoken. Candle flames flickered off the walls, illuminating a sickening sight. Instruments lay on a tray of various sizes and shapes. Next to that, a glass tank full of tiny snakes. Music blared from speakers overhead, a dance tune. And then the bathroom door opened. In walked Shek wearing a robe, open, and nothing more. He gracefully extended his hand to her, then touched her hair.

"You cut your hair. You did that so you would not be as appealing to any potential buyer."

She looked into his eyes and saw pure evil. Not an ounce of humanity. A quake her in her gut began to grip her entire body, even as she tried to fight it off and will her brain to function. To look for any opportunity to escape from this torture.

"We know you are special, Cai Chen."

Her breathing stopped.

He smiled as he stroked her short, choppy hair. "You have special skills, and those in Beijing would give almost anything to take you into custody and throw you into a detention camp. Perhaps you could join the Uyghurs," he said with a hissing chuckle. "But I have other plans for you, Cai Chen. You will be mine. Tonight, tomorrow night. And every night after. You will be my personal assistant. My pet."

He moved to the tray and ran his hand across the instruments like a concert pianist would to his beloved ivory keys of a grand piano. Her eyes shifted for a split second to a candle sitting on a nearby table.

"So," he said, turning his back to her, "we have one order of business to complete before the games begin." He turned around and slipped some type of gold jewelry onto his right hand. "You see this? It's the shape of a snake. A symbol of power that is unequaled in this region."

Realizing the so-called jewelry was nothing more than brass knuckles, she started to back up a step, but he gripped her arm.

"Your punishment for cutting your hair will be one strike. That is all. It will be your reminder to never cross me again. Let us get this behind us and then have some fun, no?"

He winked at her and then threw a straight punch into her face. She tried to dodge the punch, but it still connected with her cheekbone. She went airborne—it felt like her face had shattered, the pain unworldly. She slammed into a dresser but quickly tried to stand. Her equilibrium was off, and she dropped like a boxer who'd just been knocked out.

Shek hissed and chuckled again as he tossed his robe onto the bed and rearranged his metal instruments.

Cai had only seconds to act. She crawled three feet to the table, grabbed the candle, and lunged for Shek. He turned at the last second, and she rammed the lit flame and wax into his eye. He shrieked, dropped onto the bed, and threw his face into his robe.

Tripping at first, Cai got to her feet and stumbled to the door, opened it, and raced down the hall. She heard voices downstairs, including that of Mogwai.

"In here."

She turned. A young man about her age waved her into a room. "You need to hide and then escape later. I know where you can go."

50

Penha Hill, Macau

As Jet whistled a tune from the driver's seat of the Spada, Su and I were all business in the back. We were in the final prep stages before engaging in a surveillance operation on the estate of Xela Chang.

Su finished covering her face with black paint and handed me the canister. I used the reflection on the side window to be sure I adequately coated my face.

"Look at me," Su said, then shook her head.

"What did I miss?"

She swiped her finger in the black paint and then rubbed some on the tip of my nose.

"How did I miss that?"

"Not sure. But you have a very white nose. I do not want that snowball to grab the attention of any wandering eyes at Viper Lounge."

Viper Lounge was our nickname for Xela Chang's four-acre estate nestled in the trees on Penha Hill, about a mile up the incline from Robinson's place.

Su opened a small chest, packed away the black paint, and slipped on her Velcro watch. The watch strap was camouflage, just like our long-sleeve T-shirts and pants. She'd informed me that wearing attire to blend in with the surroundings was far more effective than dressing in all black, even at night. Apparently, black clothes could create noticeable silhouettes moving in the darkness. I, of course, acted like that was old news.

After removing two pistols, she shut the chest and locked it, then snapped at Jet. "What are you whistling?"

"I like it."

"Well, I do not."

"That's the name of the song. 'I Like It.' One of Cardi B's kick-ass tunes. It rocks."

She ignored his comment and asked, "Have you checked in with Angelique?"

He held up his phone so we could see it.

"Are you expecting us to read the screen? Come on, Jet, this is not a time to be glib or to screw around."

I asked, "Did Angelique get the girls settled at her sister's place?"

Her sister was an ER doctor. Fortunately, the bullet had only grazed Liang's head. Angelique's sister was able to treat the wound without admitting her to the hospital. Which was positive news, considering our current lack of trust in any public institution.

"Sure did," Jet said. "Unlike my dump, her sister has a nice high-rise condo in Taipa. She ordered in food, and the girls are all watching a movie in her media room."

"What about security?"

"Full security system in her condo, and a private security

firm on site."

"Glad to hear it."

Su picked up her phone and glanced at the screen.

I asked if she'd heard back from Ubaldo yet. She'd texted him earlier to let him know about Wen.

"Not after he sent me his one-word reply: *busy*."

She set the phone aside and picked up one of the pistols. "In all of your missions, have you ever had the privilege of using the chosen pistol of the People's Liberation Army?"

I shook my head. Not something I could lie about.

Su removed the magazine. "The QSZ-92 magazine holds fifteen rounds. I am hopeful that neither of us needs to fire a single bullet. Reconnaissance only, correct?" She arched her eyebrows.

"Correct. But we never discussed what the plan will be if we actually find Cai there."

"It is not going to happen, Jack. First, we want to try to verify that Xela is indeed Viper. Take pictures of anything that moves. Then the three of us reconvene at the bottom of the hill and share our findings. That will determine what happens next."

"Such as abducting a certain someone and drilling them for details of the operation, including where they took Cai."

"Exactly. Might be Shek, or maybe the grand dame herself."

"And you're still open to going back in and extracting Cai after we regroup and discuss?"

"I told you I was earlier, right?"

Something about her comment didn't sound authentic, but I just went with it. "Yep."

"Now, back to the best mass-produced pistol in the world. The barrel rotates on recoil to lock and unlock itself from the slide. An effective firing range of fifty meters. I am nearly perfect from twice that, but those are in ideal conditions. Not at night." She grabbed my hand and set the gun in my palm. "Seven hundred sixty grams. Get used to the weight. It is a little different than that peashooter you had a few days ago."

I moved my hand along the weapon, acclimated myself to the weight, then took hold of the grip. It felt good in my hands. But I knew the feel of the gun meant very little if I couldn't test it out on a firing range. And that wasn't in the cards.

"I saw night-vision goggles in your little fun box," I said.

"They will only bog us down. Plus, once we reach the main house, we will be dealing with lights. So, no need."

Su tapped her ear, and we all tested our comms devices.

Jet pulled to a stop on the upward bend of the main road with no other cars in sight, and the side door slid open. Su patted Jet's seat. "Do not park your car and sit around waiting for our signal. Stay on the move. We do not know where cameras are located or which agencies could be involved. Do not trust anyone except us. Got it?"

"I'm all in, Commander."

As he drove off, Su and I climbed into the brush and began our ascent.

51

Xela Chang Estate
Penha Hill, Macau

When I first saw the man by the pool house, I was convinced it was Spike. I could only see the back of him, but he was about the same height and width, equal to two normal-sized men. The man-beast turned around. Even from a good forty feet away, I could see the rings through this man's nose. Not an accessory Spike wore.

"Got eyes on him, Jack?" Su asked through the comms.

"I see him. Is he alone?"

"Not sure. Can you check out the entire pool area?"

"Can do. Give me a minute."

As the large man turned and ambled along the stone fencing toward the east, I moved just slightly below the stone wall in the opposite direction. The terrain was unforgiving—prickly bushes tearing at exposed skin, roots and rocks sticking out of uneven ground. On the ascent to the property, I'd tripped and fallen four times. It didn't help that we were navigating the hillside in near darkness.

After lowering myself under a web of tangled vines, I bear-crawled across a bed of loose rocks and hid behind some brush, still about twenty feet below the stone wall. I could see a cabana, one of its flaps whipping in the gusty wind, and on the far side, what looked like a small pool house. I couldn't see the pool just yet, but the back of the mansion itself was impressive. Impeccable white stucco exterior, four levels. Massive windows, revealing red and silver dragons floating near the ceiling, a contemporary art display. The home of a woman with money and power.

I had one focus: determine if Cai Chen was being held captive anywhere on this property. While I'd promised Su to treat this as a reconnaissance operation, I'd break that pledge in a heartbeat if I got eyes on the young girl who was the ticket to me reuniting with Anna and Maddie.

"Su, I don't see any other—" I'd spoken to soon. Two men in dark uniforms walked out of the mansion onto the patio.

"Jack, are you okay?"

"I'm here."

"What do you see?"

I gave her a brief description, adding, "Both have semi-automatic rifles."

"See a badge of any kind?"

I squinted for a clearer view. "Negative." I could practically hear the gears in Su's mind cranking. "What are you thinking?"

"I need to see them. Give me a minute to make my way to your position."

"Not necessary. They're taking the same path as the guy with the nose ring."

A beat of silence, then, "I just saw him walk to the east side of the patio and then he moved out of sight, going north along the side. Give me a minute to observe the two uniformed men and get back to you."

My patience bucket was running low—I had to keep moving. I noticed a balcony rimmed the west side of the home. If I could climb over the stone wall, then I could scoot around the side undetected. From there, I should be able to assess points of entry to the home.

I began a slow climb up the hill, heading toward the wall. If someone were casually glancing out a window, I didn't want them to see sudden movement. The response from those protecting the chief administrator, the person we believed ran Viper, could be swift and deadly.

I stepped over a rotting tree, then waded through thigh-high vines and bushes before stopping behind a large boulder. A faint thumping bass—loud music coming from inside the home. The patio was clear of people, and Su had yet to provide her feedback on the two unis.

I continued my trek. The hill became steeper, and I had to use my hands to keep balance and pull me along before reaching a cluster of trees, no more than ten feet below the wall. At least two of the trees soared thirty feet high, their foliage draping over the patio.

If I were a monkey, the trees would be the perfect means to get to the patio in quick order. But I was no monkey. I continued my methodical climb.

"Jack, stop where you are right now!" Su said in my ear. "The whole complex is surrounded by a thin wire that could trigger an alarm."

I looked down. A wire pressed against my thigh.

52

Shoes shuffled along the patio just above me. I didn't breathe, didn't move. A man spoke in Portuguese, and I listened intently. I'd taken Spanish back in high school, so I hoped to at least be able to pick out a familiar word or phrase.

I got the sense he was speaking to someone on a phone or a comms device. A pause, then more Portuguese. I heard *gringo* and *claro*. I was a *gringo*—a white man. *Claro* meant clear. All clear of the white man? It was impossible to decipher a thousand-word statement with only two words to go on.

The shoes shuffled away.

I carefully pulled my leg away from the wire and released a breath. "Thanks for the warning, Su. How did you know I'd moved up the hill closer to the stone wall?"

"Because I did the same thing."

"You broke your own rule."

"You are more impatient than I am, so I was worried. Turns out I was right."

I could have argued that fact, but now wasn't the time. I crouched lower and eyed the thin wire. "Just one wire, do you think?"

"I did a quick inspection on my side—just one wire. Your side could be different. This wire is a smart move by someone who wants an additional layer of security on top of the manpower."

"Did you ID the men in the uniforms?"

"Saw no badge or any type of insignia. I think they are private security. Weapons were Chinese military, the QBZ-95. It is possible they are former military, or this is a side job. Maybe one that pays quite well."

While she was speaking, I'd dipped under the wire and continued my final push to the wall. I peeked in between two stone balustrades. The illuminated aqua pool water glistened as the wind kicked up ripples. No sign of guards, uniformed or not.

"Did you hear me, Jack?"

"I heard you." No one was looking out the windows of the home, as far as I could tell. I slipped over the wall.

Su said, "I have cleared the wire trap, and now I am about to climb onto the patio. I plan to go around the east side of house to get a better look at anyone inside. Sorry I did not share this plan with you earlier. Given my military background, I am better equipped for this."

"I get it." And I wasn't waiting. I crept toward the west side of the house and spotted a downspout that led to a second-story balcony and an open door.

"You stay on the hill and keep your eyes on the house," Su said. "Let me know if you see anyone headed in my direction."

"Will do." If she was going rogue, then she'd just have to deal with me doing the same. I tugged on the gutter—there was no give—and climbed up the wall until my hand touched the balcony.

A man's voice from above. I turned into stone with one hand still gripping the gutter. He spoke in Cantonese, and I couldn't understand a damn word. But the voice was measured. Precise. I'd only heard one voice like that during my time in Macau.

It was Shek.

My hand on the gutter was exposed, but I feared if I pulled it off, Shek would see movement. He was a slight man. I guessed no more than five-six, a buck fifty. But he had power. I knew in my gut he would wield his power in a way that would be just as measured and precise as his voice. And decisive.

I tilted my head. He was speaking on a phone, the pulsating bass of dance music playing in the background. Perspiration trickled down my forehead and stopped at the tip of my nose. An annoyance, but one I'd gladly accept if I could escape this predicament undetected.

Shek turned so that his body was now facing me. He shuffled forward, his shoes only inches from the tips of my fingers. As he spoke into the phone, he gazed across the complex. I took a quick breath. Just one. I was losing my grip on the balcony, and my arm that was outstretched to the gutter felt like it might snap at the shoulder. I couldn't hold on much longer.

Commit to the balcony, or go back to the gutter? Either way, he would see me and sic the man-beast army on me. The wind kicked up, and sand flew into my eyes. The grit clawed at my eyelids, but I could do nothing about it.

Shek stopped speaking. I braced myself for him to shout, "Intruder!" or stomp my hand. But he didn't. A few more words in Cantonese, then he pocketed the phone and walked inside the mansion.

I swung my hand from gutter to balcony, briefly swiping at my eyes in the process. I gathered myself and pulled upward until I reached the railing. A better view inside. No sign of Shek or anyone else. Only a stone statue of Buddha staring back at me.

I put a knee on the edge of the balcony, then over the railing I went in one smooth motion, my eyes focused on the room before me, doors still open.

A man walked through the far end of the room, disappearing out a side door. Something flashed in his hand. A knife? Not certain of the weapon. But I was certain of the person. Wen.

I stepped toward the Buddha statue…

A scream in my ear.

"Su? You there?"

Muffled voices. The sounds of a struggle. Su grunting?

"Su!"

A pop made my breath hitch. Two more gunshots. "Su!"

Back to the railing. I swung my legs over, shimmied down the gutter, jumping the last ten feet to the ground.

"Su!" I repeated two, three, four times.

No response.

I pulled my pistol from my holster and raced to the back of the house. Saw no one. Ran past the enormous windows, thought I saw movement inside, but I didn't dare take my eyes off the far side of the house. But when I passed the pool, I did a double take.

Something was floating along the top.

A blue cap.

Rounding the corner to the east side of the house, I almost stumbled over the body. A guard. Blood pooled around his head. A hole just above his right eye that was staring back at me. Lifeless.

It seemed Su had won the battle. But where was she? I grabbed the dead man's gun and tossed it into the brush.

People were yelling now, someone barking out orders. I had to find Su and hope we could escape before a battalion of armed guards engulfed the entire compound. I thought of Wen. He was neck-deep in this scheme. What did he know about Cai Chen?

The voices grew louder. I ran down the side of the house and found a door ajar. I gently pushed it open. A library with a rolling ladder that reached the top shelves. I stepped inside. There was a door that led to a hallway, and I started in that direction.

A gun barrel pressed against the side of my head.

“Move and you’re dead.”

53

The angle of the gun, the sound of the voice. One thing was clear: a very large man stood to my right.

"Put the gun on the floor."

I did as he said. The barrel never left the side of my head.

"Should I kill you right here?"

"No need. I can leave. I'll jump over the fence and—"

He smacked the gun against my skull. I almost toppled over as tiny motes of light danced around me.

"Tired of your shit. At Robinson's party. At the jockey club."

It was Spike. A vengeful Spike.

"I can pay you."

"Bah! Not as much as I'm making now. But as much as I want to kill you, I can't. Shek will chew my ass if I spill blood on this fine rug."

"You don't want to kill anyone. Just let me—"

"Walk." He tapped my bruised head with the barrel.

I stepped deeper into the library, searching for a diversion or a weapon. My eyes locked on a brass candlestick sitting on a nearby table. No way I'd have enough time to lunge toward the table and swing the candlestick at Spike.

When we reached the threshold of the door on the opposite side of the library, the hallway stretched a good thirty feet in front of me, a T at the end. Numerous doorways lined both sides. The thumping bass of the dance music persisted—my pulse matched the rapid rhythm.

A flash of people ran across the hallway at the T. Su at the front. A beat behind her was the man with the nose ring, holding a pistol and laughing.

"Get her, bro!" When Spike cupped his hand to shout, the gun pulled back from my head. Not much. But I didn't need much.

I swung my elbow into his gun hand, quickly followed by a straight punch to his nose. He yelped, staggered a couple of steps, but never dropped the gun. I spun on my heels, lunged for the first open door, but Spike clipped my foot. With my arms outstretched, I dropped hard, slamming my face off the floor. I started to push up to my elbows and knees, but a boot the size of a toolbox rammed into my kidney. Back on the floor, gasping for air.

"Shek can take the damage out of my pay."

I peered upward, wincing. Spike smiled, showing his black teeth, and moved the barrel of the gun within two feet of my head. I swung my leg straight up—a direct hit to his jewels. He went cross-eyed, released a high-pitched yelp. The gun went off. I flinched. The bullet slammed into the floor under my armpit. A second later, Spike fell on top of me. Growling like the beast he was, he put two hands on the gun and tried to bring it up. But my two hands were pulling in the opposite direction. His strength, even in his weakened state, was a power I'd never encountered. And with each second, that power grew. His smile returned, and so did a menacing laughter. An animal about to devour its prey.

With a final surge, Spike turned the gun, the barrel pressing against my chest. His disgusting fish breath engulfed my body. The laughter reached a fever pitch—I was nearly out of time. But I still had one last trick. I cocked my head backward, then rammed it with everything I had into Spike's nose. Cartilage crunched like broken walnuts. He released the gun, covered his bloody nose with his hands, screaming as he rolled to the side. I scooped up the gun and shot him in the chest. Twice.

Footfalls approached the room, and I lifted the gun. Su pulled to a stop, looked at Spike, then me. "I'm going after Xela." She sped away in the opposite direction.

I took a few breaths, grabbed a pillow, and wiped Spike's blood off my face, then moved carefully into the long hallway. My heart pumped like I was ascending Mount Everest, but the goal never wavered. Find Cai Chen. If she wasn't on the property, then get to Shek and threaten him until he tells me where she was.

One foot into the hallway, there was shouting at the far end. A blur of people raced along the T at the end of the hallway. One, maybe two guards. Su might have been at the front of the line.

I pressed my earbud. "Su, you okay?"

No response.

Gun raised, I ran toward the end of the hall, glancing into each open room I passed. At the T, I looked left. Huge windows overlooking the pool, a tranquil backdrop compared to the hell breaking loose inside. I hustled down the hall, my entire body feeling as though I'd been tasered.

I stopped when the corridor spilled into a kitchen. On the other side of the kitchen was a dining room with glass chandeliers and an expansive living room with ten-foot paintings on the walls.

I stepped onto the glossy tile. Movement off to my right. By the time I swung my gun in that direction, a barrel had come around the side of one of the doorways. An orange flash. I dove for cover. Splinters of wood were like daggers in my face. I squeezed my eyes shut and kept rolling until I rammed into the center island.

When I looked up, a man in a blue uniform was coming around the island, gun in hand. A woman with dangling diamond earrings in a blue silk dress was moving behind him.

Xela, trying to escape.

I lifted my pistol and fired a single round, blowing a chunk out of the guy's shoulder. He cried out but kept coming. I fired two more shots—one to the chest, the other piercing his chin. He flipped around, firing his gun indiscriminately, then fell straight over. I kicked his gun away and rose to one knee. Xela was on the floor, blood draining from her mouth.

I scrambled to her side. "Tell me where you have Cai Chen."

Nothing. Her eyes didn't blink. She was dead.

Fuck.

The thumping bass was just as loud but faster. It was coming from upstairs. A staircase at the far side of the living room. I raced out of the kitchen but quickly paused and did a quick gut check. Something seemed off.

Anxious that I'd missed my chance to interrogate Xela? Close to finding Cai? What? I couldn't pin it down.

I bounded up the steps two at a time, all stealth. On the second floor, I peered into the closest room. It was vacant, unless someone was hiding under the bed. No time for a thorough inspection. I moved down the hall, which spilled into a bar area that opened up to downstairs. I peered over the railing. No movement from below.

But I did hear laughter. From one of rooms on this floor. I tilted my head and heard it again. It might be part of the music.

But it might also be a person.

I moved to the wall and shuffled toward the open doorway. I counted to three and took a lightning-quick peek. Red sheer curtains fluttered from a stiff breeze through an open window. It was a suite, with a partial wall separating the bedroom area.

Crouching low, I pulled around the corner. No bullets, a good sign. I heard a cackle from the other side of the partial wall. I darted behind a chair and paused. No visual of the person. I shifted to the next object, a large chest. One eye around it—the partial wall was actually a large fireplace, its opening covered by an ornate gold screen. Painted in red was a hissing snake.

A viper.

I took the risk and moved behind the fireplace. On my way, there was a flash of metal from the other side. Someone was waving an object. My mind started piecing together images. When I heard the laughter again, I jumped around the fireplace with my gun raised.

"Knife down, Wen!"

His back was to me. He had a grip of Ubaldo's hair, the knife raised.

"Wen. Put the knife down and turn around."

He rotated to face me. Smiling, maniacal, unhinged.

"Mr. Jack Whitfield. Lots of people are looking for you and Su." He released Ubaldo with a shove and tapped the flat edge of the blade against his hand.

Ubaldo's face was a bloody mess. One eye was shut. The other was wide open. Nothing but fear.

"Why'd you do it, Wen?"

He brought a finger to the edge of his mouth and smirked. "Oh, what do you mean?" He threw his head back and laughed.

"You beat up your best friend. Why? For money?"

"Screw off. You killed my brother. Ubaldo here did not like that I wanted revenge. So, he got a one-way ticket to hell."

"The girls. Why did you try to kill the girls?"

"That was for money. Shek and Xela ask me to do things."

"You don't care about your friend? You don't care how they sell those girls like cattle?"

"I guess you did not hear me say it was for money. Mostly. It is also about honor and revenge. Too bad you have that gun on me. I could show you a couple of tricks with my knife. Why don't you toss the gun to the side and we go a couple of rounds?"

"Put the knife down."

He shook his head. "Not sure how you got out of those drug charges."

He'd planted the drugs in my room. Fury rose within me, but I maintained a cool exterior. He chuckled and took a step toward me.

"No closer. Drop the knife, then face down on the floor. Do it!"

"Maybe I don't feel like it." He moved another step closer.

"Wen, this isn't going to end well for you if you move another inch. I won't hesitate to shoot you."

A stare-down ensued. I didn't blink. Finally, he tossed the knife on the bed and dropped to his knees.

"Ubaldo, you with me?" I moved closer, and he moaned a bit. His wrists and ankles were zip-tied, so I grabbed the knife and cut him free. All the while making sure Wen didn't move from his position on the floor.

"Need to get you to a hospital." I spoke into my comms. "Su, are you out there? I found Ubaldo."

No response. I helped Ubaldo to his feet.

Wen snarled, his eyes on Ubaldo. "You know I will find her, right? Nothing will stop me."

I stopped in my tracks, my arm around Ubaldo's waist. "Find who?"

"Just some little wench. Worth top dollar."

"Is that why you were torturing Ubaldo? Dude, you're going to jail."

He cackled. "Yeah, right. Do you know who my boss is? Good chance you don't get off this property alive. Been nice knowing you. Looking forward to spitting on your dead body."

When I rounded the fireplace, Su walked into the room. I said, "Hey there."

"Down!" She swung her gun upward. I lunged to my right, taking Ubaldo with me.

Shots echoed throughout the room.

54

Wen cried out and fell to the floor, unmoving.

I saw blood—Ubaldo's blood.

Su shouted, "Oh God, Ubaldo!" She dropped to her knees and pulled him to her. He'd been shot in the back. Wen had pulled a pistol hidden in his sock and fired on his old friend.

As she rocked Ubaldo in her arms, I pressed my fingers against his neck. Nothing. I glanced at Wen sprawled across the floor, checked him. Also dead.

I got to my knees, unsure what to say or do. Su wept quietly and held her cousin close. Aside from her sobs, it was quiet. A wayward bullet must have pierced the sound system.

Unsure of what dangers still lurked outside of this room, I peeked into the hallway. I wondered who was alive, who had escaped, and if anyone still on the grounds might know where Cai Chen was.

I returned to Su's side, resting a reassuring hand on her shoulder. She kissed Ubaldo's forehead and gently laid him on the floor.

"I'm so sorry, Su. I know your goal was to take Ubaldo away from all this."

Her chest lifted as she wiped her eyes. "I called my backup team."

"MSS?"

She nodded. "Should be on site within minutes."

I debated leaving before the MSS agents arrived. I asked Su what she'd seen and if we should be concerned about other dangers on the property.

"I think we are clear. Shek escaped with his guard—the one with the nose ring. I shot the guard in the arm. We should collect Wen's gun."

I grabbed the gun and stood up straight, stretching my aching muscles but prepared to act.

Su tilted her head and got very still.

"What do you hear? Is it MSS?" I worried how my interaction with the MSS agents would go down. Might be time to exit this place, on my own.

"No. It seems like… Do you hear that?" Su moved to her knees and turned her head, apparently trying to zero in on the origin of the sound.

"What exactly?"

"Sounds like a mouse or something. But not really."

She wasn't making much sense, but I focused hard to hear this mysterious sound. Several seconds later, I heard the noise—like a whimpering puppy. "I think it's coming from—"

"The fireplace."

I got to my feet and pulled on the fireplace screen. It was bolted to the stone hearth. I felt around the edge for a way to release it. Su joined me. "These bastards are the sickest people on earth," I said. "Trying to suffocate a dog inside a fireplace… Su?"

Her face was all scrunched up. Concentration? Concern? Probably both. I wasn't sure she'd even heard me.

"Hey, I have to be honest. I'm going to take off before your MSS friends show up."

"Hush."

"Huh?"

She pointed at the fireplace. "I think there is someone inside."

"A dog."

She shook her head. "A person."

55

"Hold on, okay?" Su said after knocking on the screen. "We will get you out."

We pawed furiously at the edges but made no headway. I sat back on my heels, examined the craftsmanship involved in creating the screen, how they'd put it together. *I wonder...*

I raced to the other side of the fireplace. Hand screws protruded from the screen. "Su! I've got it."

She ran over and worked on the bottom two screws, while I tackled the top. In less than sixty seconds, I'd pulled the screen away.

A girl covered in soot rolled out, coughing, gagging. I caught her, lifted her to standing. She looked like Cai, but I wasn't sure. "Are you…?"

She coughed in my face.

I turned to Su. "Can you get a wet cloth and water?"

Su ran into an adjoining bathroom. When I pulled matted hair from the girl's mouth, I realized her hair was only shoulder-length and uneven. The photo of Cai showed her hair was much longer, more than halfway down her back. "How long have you been in there?"

Su handed the girl a glass of water and a wet towel. Through coughing fits, she managed to drink the entire glass. Su went to get her a refill while the girl used the towel to wipe her eyes. After her second glass of water, she took a moment to study us.

"What's your name?" I asked.

Her eyes continued to volley between us. Su said, "I am with the government. You are safe. We know you were being held captive by bad people. Did they try to sell you to someone?"

She nodded. "I was in a ship with many other girls. Some were killed by…by this monster."

"Mogwai," I said.

Her eyes filled with tears. She quickly ran the cloth across her face and seethed. "And Shek. He was even worse."

"How long have they kept you in that fireplace?"

Her brown eyes dropped to the floor.

Su glanced at me, then patted the girl's back. "You can feel safe. We have most of them in custody now. We will soon get the others. You have no reason to be fearful. We will reunite you with your family."

The girl bit into her lip, and a tear slid down her cheek. She had to be suffering from PTSD, just like Liang and Huan.

"You can tell us what happened, or wait and talk to your family," Su said.

The girl's eyes shifted to Wen's motionless body. "That person was trying to find me."

"Wen? You know him?" Su asked.

She shook her head. "I escaped from Shek, looking for a place to hide. And then Ubaldo found me."

"Ubaldo?" Su said with a gasp.

"When I was running from everyone, Ubaldo found a hiding

spot for me." She nudged her head toward the fireplace. "He saved my life. He gave up his life for mine. I owe him so much."

Su grabbed the girl, and they held each other, sobbing. I pulled out my phone and compared the girl in front of me with the photo of Cai. When they finally parted, I asked her, "What is your name?"

She arched her back. "Cai Chen."

I heard the name, but it took a few seconds for it to fully register. When it did, my adrenaline spiked. So much so that my phone slipped from my hand onto the floor. She handed it to me.

"Thank you, Cai." I thought about sharing this watershed moment with Su—how I'd reached my mission's endgame—but it was too soon. I had to wait until I had Anna and Maddie in my arms. I turned my back to them and typed out a quick text to Simon:

Good news! I found Cai Chen. She's here with me. Viper is now exposed. MSS to shut it down.

After I tapped send, a smile spread across my face. Some of the tension in my shoulders and back started to subside. My phone dinged, and I viewed the text:

Send a picture.

That made sense. I snapped a couple of quick shots while the ladies chatted, then sent one to Simon.

Su noticed. "Jack, what's that about?"

I shook my head and stared at the screen, waiting. Another ding, just as Su's phone did the same.

I read the text and suddenly felt lightheaded.

Get to a safe spot and reach out to us. She cannot be harmed. We need her to do some important work for us.

"Jack, agents just arrived. I am going to meet them. Bring Cai downstairs, please."

My mind swirling, I read the text on my phone one more time.

"Jack, did you hear me?"

"Uh, yeah. Just give me a second."

"Do not be long, please. I want us to explain everything together…and provide assistance with Cai if needed. And then they need to help me with Ubaldo."

Su disappeared out of the room, and Cai moved closer to me. "Something is wrong?"

"Uh…" My hand that held the phone quivered until I pulled my arm against my chest. I studied Cai, then my phone, and back to Cai. "Who are you?"

"Cai Chen."

"No, I mean, why are you so important to Xela, Shek, this whole sleazy crowd?"

Her eyes dropped to the floor.

"What's wrong?"

She opened her mouth for a second but didn't speak.

I could hear voices downstairs, and I turned toward the door for a second, then back to Cai. "Please tell me. I was sent halfway across the world to rescue you."

"I am a wanted person."

"For what?"

"Cybercrime. The Chinese government believes I am one of the preeminent hackers in the world."

"You're a hacker," I said, the dots connecting to Simon's text. I looked at my phone and mumbled, "But why would Simon want me to find a hacker?"

"Who is Simon?"

The voices became louder. I took her by the hand. "We need to get the hell off this property."

Footfalls on the stairs. I led her down the hallway, searching for the room with the Buddha statue. "Here." I shut the door behind us and gestured for her to stand behind me. Seconds later, a rush of people hurried along the hallway past our position.

"Follow me." I ran past the Buddha statue, over to the balcony door, and took a step out onto the ledge. When I turned around, Cai was still in the room. I waved her on. She shook her head. I raced back to her side.

"What's wrong?"

"I have been held captive. I have had my freedom taken away. I am not sure I want to go with you."

We had no time for this. "Cai, I know you've been scared. It makes sense. But you need to trust me." I grabbed her hand again and began to walk toward the balcony. She pulled away, her feet unmoving.

Shouting in the hallway. The MSS agents were looking for us. And if they found us—found *me*—I might be interrogated for thirty straight days. And that was the best-case scenario.

"Cai, I can't make you come with me. That's not what we do back in the States."

Now she looked perplexed. "Why are you doing this? You are not with the MSS."

"You're right. I…" I bit my tongue, unsure of how much to share. The floor shook from pounding footsteps. The agents were making their way through the upstairs rooms. I had no idea if Su was one of them or what could be going through her mind right now.

"Cai, I must leave. I can't be caught up in bureaucracy with the MSS or any other government agency. The lives of my wife and daughter are on the line."

"Your wife and daughter?"

"I'll tell you everything about why I'm here, why I was looking for you, how my family is at the center of all of it. But we don't have time right now. Let's get out of here, and I'll share it all."

She set her jaw and nodded. "I will go with you."

We raced through the door, out to the balcony stone wall.

"How are we supposed to get to the ground?" she asked.

I gauged her weight. Probably no more than a hundred pounds. "Wrap your arms around my shoulders."

I climbed over the railing, and she locked her arms around my neck. Her wrists pulled against my Adam's apple, but we didn't have time to work out the details. I grabbed the gutter and set my feet against the side of the house. The metal screeched, pulling away from the wall a few inches.

"Hold on." I hustled down the gutter in quick order. Eight feet from the ground, the entire downspout broke free from the house. I twisted midair, allowing my knees to absorb most of the impact.

We got to our feet, and I took Cai's hand. We raced along the side of the house, heading toward the back wall of the property. "Stop! Come back here!" a man yelled from behind us.

A gunshot made us lurch and stumble. But neither of us had been hit. Just as we regained our footing, there was another pop.

And Cai dropped like a hand from hell had just thrown her down.

56

"Cai!"

Skidding to a stop on my knees, I placed a hand on her back. She didn't move for two agonizing seconds—long enough for me to realize how everything in my life depended on keeping her safe. She quickly pushed herself up to standing, looking over her shoulder. She'd tripped over a planter. "I am fine. Come on."

She was on the move and pumping her arms before I'd taken a full breath. We made it to the back of the house, jumped over someone's unmoving body. We'd temporarily found cover.

"Mogwai," she muttered while peering down at the lifeless body.

"Bastard's dead."

She scanned the area. "How do we get out of here?"

"Over the back wall. I know the way."

We scooted around the cabana, rimmed the pool, and made our way to the far wall. Trees and the steep hillside were just beyond, nothing more than a dark abyss. More yelling from outside the house. I tensed, realizing there could be a dozen or more MSS agents searching for us.

I started to give Cai instructions while helping over the wall, but she swatted my hand away.

"I got it." She scooted over the wall, paused, then jumped for the tree, landing on a sturdy branch. With my adrenaline spigot still fully open, I bounced in place as I waited for her move out of the way. Just before I leaped, I took one more look toward the mansion. MSS agents were rushing out the door.

"Crap!" I made the jump and let the branches break my fall on the way to the ground. Dozens of puncture wounds, but I was still in one piece. I told Cai about the MSS agents closing in on us, and we started stumbling our way down the hill. Though I was somewhat familiar with the landscape, it didn't take long for Cai to scurry past me.

"You done much hiking?"

"Not in the dark," she said, scampering down the hill.

A second later, we were bathed in light. People shouting just behind us. I raised a hand to ward off the glare of a spotlight bearing down on us. They hadn't pegged us just yet, but it wouldn't be long.

"Behind the brush over there," I told Cai, pointing. She nodded, and we covered the short distance in seconds. The thicket of bushes and weeds blocked most of the spotlight. "Let's keep going but stay low to the ground. Hope they won't see us."

Leading the way, I traversed over a boulder, then…

My foot clipped something that moved. I went flying headfirst into some type of prickly bush a good twenty feet down the hill. A breath and a quick assessment. Nothing broken. When I lifted to my knees, I caught the silhouette of arms swinging in the darkness.

"Cai!" I raced up the hill toward her.

She was punching and kicking Shek. I'd tripped over him. As

I pulled out my gun, Shek spun Cai right into me. The pistol fell from my grip as she and I tumbled to the ground. He scooped up the gun just as I got to my feet. He started hissing and laughing, a repulsive sound.

"I need Cai for my ticket to freedom. But you? I will take pleasure in ending your life right now."

From the ground, Cai swung a baton-sized branch into his shin. He howled and bucked straight back. The gun fired into the night as his back hit the turf. I grabbed the gun and pointed it at him. But before I could say a word, Cai snatched it from my grip and fired two shots into his chest. And then one more into his face.

For a few seconds, Cai didn't move, the gun still pointing at Shek, but I could hear her hissing out breaths.

The spotlight hit us. Then, more yelling.

"They know where we are. Let's go!" I said. We covered ground like goats on speed. Within thirty seconds, I spotted the path I'd taken from the road. "Down here."

We hustled along the narrow path, jumping the final four feet onto the road. Only seconds before agents would be upon us. What now? It was the middle of the night on a lonely road on Penha Hill.

"I hope you can jog," I said.

And we jogged, heading around the long bend in the road. No sign of MSS agents. Not yet, at least.

"Might take us ten minutes or so to wind our way to the bottom of the hill. But I remembered some small homes along the way. Maybe we can cut through their yards, shave off some time."

"Okay."

A horn blared, and tires bit the asphalt. A car stopped not ten feet in front of us. The headlights were so severe I couldn't tell if it was a police car or some other government agency vehicle or just some regular guy out for a nighttime drive.

The door opened.

"Get behind me." I stood in front of Cai, knowing we couldn't outrun a car.

"Mr. Whitfield! It's me."

"Jet?"

"Just your friendly taxi service."

I started walking toward him but realized that Cai was not. "It's okay. I know him. He's a good guy."

She looked doubtful but pulled up alongside me. Jet looked at her, then at me—questioning.

I said, "Don't ask. And don't call Su. Just drive, okay?"

He gave me a mock salute and got into the front seat. Cai and I slid into the back. Jet turned the car around and started the descent. "Where should I drive, Mr. Whitfield?"

"That's your name?" Cai asked before I could reply to Jet.

"First name is Jack. Jet, go anywhere away from this hill."

"Roger that. And what do I say if the commander calls?"

Cai gave me a strange look.

"He's talking about Su, the nice woman you met in the mansion."

"Nice?" Jet said.

Cai seemed concerned, but I tried to give her some perspective. "Su is pretty intense at times, but she's a good person." I immediately questioned my use of the phrase "good person." Was Su one of the agents chasing us? Could be. Best to view her as a possible enemy for now.

Jet's phone rang. His stressed face told me it was the commander herself. He said, "What do I tell her?"

"Don't answer it. When she asks you later, tell her your phone died, whatever. But I hope to keep you out of this, Jet. Just need a few minutes to think."

Which I did.

I looked at Cai and said, "First, I need to tell you what this is all about. I promised you that much."

57

Macau

The older section of Macau, the one rooted in Portuguese culture, was active yet subdued, allowing our Spada to blend in with the cars and people, all busy trying to stay afloat. While survival was also at the top of my list—especially with the MSS searching for us—I was eager to learn what Simon wanted us to do for what hopefully would be our final task.

I smacked my dry lips as I checked my phone for a message from Simon for at least the twentieth time. I'd sent them the "all safe" note and was now awaiting the instructions, what would likely be a hacking operation for Cai. In all my years competing athletically on the international stage, none had matched this type of nervous anticipation. Nervous that Cai would have the skills and desire to fulfill the request. Cautiously hopeful that Anna and Maddie were still alive and that we'd be reunited in the very near future.

I shifted my eyes to Cai, who was staring out the side window. Her eyes were pensive. I'd just shared all the gory details of how I'd gotten to this point: the abduction of Anna and Maddie, Simon's subsequent blackmail to force me to find and rescue her, Cai, and now awaiting Simon's last directive. I hoped like hell none of that had scared her off.

She finally turned to me. "I truly admire your loyalty to your family, Jack."

"I did what any father and husband would do for their two most important people in the world. I'm no one special. Anna and Maddie are the courageous ones."

As her sights shifted to the floorboard, Jet cleared his throat, then locked eyes with me through the rearview mirror. He said nothing, only giving me a nod. I could sense his understanding and his support, now after finally hearing the full truth of my motivation.

As much as it pained me, I didn't try to convince Cai of anything. I waited her out, which took at least five minutes.

"Before my father left, he taught me everything I know about hacking. How do you like that? A criminal profession." Cai sighed. "But my father and I have been separated for far too long, so I am fully aware of parents who put in the effort and of those who do not. While he occasionally pops into my life, at least virtually, I know I cannot rely on him."

"My dad is the same. Not been around much."

She nodded. "After hearing your story Jack, I will help with whatever you need me to do so you can reunite with your wife and daughter. Something good can hopefully come from this madness."

Tears began to pool in my eyes, until my phone buzzed. "The text from Simon," I said, opening the message. I blinked a hundred times as I read it.

"What is my task?" she asked.

I wiped my hand across my face, in disbelief of what they were requesting.

"Tell me, Jack. I expect the worst. Just tell me."

I shook my head. "They want you to hack into the main Chinese military data center and steal the code that manages its ICBM arsenal. Is that even possible?"

She cursed under her breath, then looked at me. "I know how to go about it. But I need to be in my computer lab."

"Where is that?"

"In a shanty in Kowloon. Can Jet take us there?"

I started to ask Jet for one last favor, but he interrupted me.

"I got this, Mr. Whitfield. I'll have you there in no time. Even better, I'll do it with my mouth shut."

58

Unknown location

Anna watched and listened every moment she was awake. For even the slightest evidence of pending danger, and for any opportunities to escape their kidnappers.

By her best estimate, she'd been awake at least forty-eight hours straight. In case there were hidden cameras, she had closed her eyes, but she had not fallen asleep. She couldn't afford to do so.

While she couldn't predict how the next steps would unfold exactly, she had taken steps to prepare herself mentally and physically, starting with securing the plastic fork. As she'd hoped, the man with the limp had forgotten about the fork on the next two tray pickups. Then on the third, he asked her about it.

"I already gave it to you," she lied. "Remember, I hid it under the plate the first time you came for the tray. I didn't want you to get in trouble." She had done her best to bond with this man, trying to bring out the compassion she'd seen a glimpse of a few times.

He'd scratched the back of his head but didn't push back. "Oh, right."

Anna had whittled the fork against the concrete floor down to a single prong, both sharp and relatively strong if she gripped the handle in just the right manner. Outside of mental fortitude, the fork was her only weapon. It was now safely hidden in the arm of Maddie's stuffed animal.

The overwhelming preference was for Anna to skillfully charm the man with the limp—no form of flattery was off the table—so that he would help them escape. But those plans took a drastic turn south during the most recent delivery of their meal. A woman had entered the room. Like her predecessor, she wore a face covering, but that was where the similarities had ended. The woman had been terse, wanting no part of any small talk. After several failed attempts, Anna had asked about the other man who brought their food.

"He is no longer responsible for you and your daughter," the woman said. "That is my job now. And if you want to stay alive, you will do as you are told and not speak to me."

Initially disheartened, Anna brushed the setback aside and increased her vigilance for any escape opportunity. And when the woman had come in to retrieve the tray, Anna spotted such an opening. It was small, but an opportunity, nonetheless. As the woman left the room with the tray in hand, Anna had noticed daylight seeping through a crack in a door across the darkened hallway. It had to be a door to the outside. She hoped that was their door to freedom.

Anna debated internally countless times in the last two days whether she should just wait out the kidnappers and hope Jack would do what needed to be done, effecting their release. On the other hand, how could she trust that these kidnappers would follow through on their end of the bargain to release them? Was Jack even still alive?

Her mind was made up. She informed Maddie of her plan and made her promise to run as fast as she could through that door across the hall, even if Mommy was not right behind her. Without any hesitation, Maddie nodded and said she would.

Anna retrieved the fork from Woofies's arm and hid it under her sleeve, then started to toss the stuffed animal playfully, drawing laughter from her daughter.

The door to their room opened, and the woman entered with the tray of food. Unlike her predecessor, she never offered a courtesy knock.

"You have ten minutes to eat and drink." As the woman lowered the tray to the floor, Anna threw Woofies into the tray—a pretend accident—sending a cup flying into the corner of the room.

"Oh, sorry," Anna said.

"Imbecile!" The woman released an audible sigh as she moved to pick up the cup.

The moment she turned her back, Anna launched from her knees, driving the plastic weapon directly into the woman's neck. Blood spurted. Maddie shrieked.

"Maddie, run like I told you! I'm right behind you."

Maddie ran for the door, and Anna followed but slipped on the woman's blood, momentarily dropping to her knees. As the woman gurgled for air behind her, Anna caught traction and bolted out of her position, racing into the hallway just as Madde had pushed through the far door. The light initially blinded Anna, and she lifted an arm.

"I'm right behind you, Maddie. Keep going!"

A second later, a human bowling ball slammed Anna into the wall.

59

Kowloon, Hong Kong

The sounds of the city never stopped, especially in Kowloon, where the populous was even denser than on the island. But for a quick moment, the horn honking and jackhammering had gone mute. It was as if I were back in Donelson and the swarm of crickets had been silenced by an enemy. Fearing that MSS agents had hunted us down, I pushed a tattered curtain to the side and peered out a clouded window of the small structure that served as Cai Chen's computer lab.

"See anyone?" Cai asked, sitting behind a desk that had held three giant monitors, three computers, two servers, and countless other surge protectors and UPS devices.

"Mostly cars in the distance, although I see a few people smoking at the bottom of the hill."

"They actually live in this shantytown. I do not know how they do it." She typed on her keyboard with remarkable swiftness and studied her left monitor, mumbling technical jargon. She'd been going at this for eight straight hours.

After dropping us off, Jet had retrieved an assortment of food—he knew a guy who operated a takeout diner that never closed. Cai ate like a woman who'd been denied food for weeks while she worked. Even as the Chinese spices filled the air, I couldn't consume food. I'd eat once Anna and Maddie were in my arms, and not a second sooner. I'd given Jet a hearty thank-you and a solid handshake and told him to get the hell out of the area so he could avoid a potential run-in with MSS agents. He had given me a bearhug and ran out of the house.

"I'm in," Cai said before typing on her keyboard.

"Do you have the code yet?" I asked, rushing to look over her shoulder. The monitors were filled with indecipherable gibberish.

"In process. Cross your fingers that their security will not boot me out before I have the code."

I didn't cross my fingers, but I paced. Five minutes turned into ten. Still going at twenty minutes, I asked myself why Simon hadn't attempted to steal this code themselves. It took me less than a minute to come up with an answer. "Simon didn't want to leave a digital trail back to its operation," I muttered.

"You are trying to figure out why Simon did not do what I am doing. I had the same answer as you." She went back to work.

"Getting any closer?"

Her head moved, but I couldn't tell the direction. "In process."

I went back to pacing, trying to tamp down the impatience, the stress. As much as I tried not to get ahead of myself, my thoughts went to Anna and Maddie. Of old times, of what they must have felt during this horrific experience, mostly of what our new future would be like. I would work less. Far less. If I didn't actively show it before, I now pledged that my family—my girls—would be my number one priority. I even found myself envisioning adding a new member to the family. A son? A second daughter? My love for all of them could fill an ocean. And I would keep them all safe.

I took in a breath at the same time my eyes landed on an egg roll. Suddenly, I felt hungry. A good sign.

There was a knock on the door.

Cai and I both lurched. "They found us!" Cai hissed, and she began to tremble.

"We can escape through the window," I said, moving in front of her.

"But I don't have the code in my sandbox yet."

Fuck!

"Jack, open the door."

Cai and I looked at each other, then I went to the door and peered through the peephole. I swung the door open, pulled Su inside, and put my gun to her temple.

"You've got ten seconds to give me a good reason not to put a bullet in your head."

"Drop the gun, Jack."

"Not a chance. Five seconds."

"Jack, Jet told me where you are."

I cursed again. "I should have never trusted him. Dammit!"

"I made him tell me where you were. MSS agents are in the area. You need to leave, find another hiding place."

I studied her as I pumped out breaths like I'd been sprinting.

"I am serious, Jack. Do you think I would turn you in? I hate the whole system. If I can somehow get out of this mess, I am going to defect."

"Why not just leave without dealing with us?"

"Jet told me the whole story. I knew this was personal for you. I want to help."

I turned to Cai. "Are you able to keep working?"

She moved back to her computer station without a word spoken.

"Can you lower your gun, please?" Su asked.

"Yeah, sorry." I walked to the lone window and looked outside. No sign of any people loitering near our shack.

"Hold on," Su said, putting a finger to her ear, apparently listening to the chatter of her MSS colleagues. She looked away, nodded a few times, then spoke to me. "They're headed right for us. Less than five minutes out."

"Cai?" I asked.

"In process."

Su moved next to me, whispering, "Do you know how much longer she needs?"

"I have a feeling she doesn't know exactly." I peered out the window again, Su looking over my shoulder.

"They could be coming from any direction, Jack, including through the roof." She pulled out her phone and stared at the screen. "Jet just said they are moving this location from up the hill. Thirty seconds, tops."

I looked to Cai. I knew she'd heard Su. Her face was stoic as she typed on her keyboard. I was about to ask her how much longer when she jumped from her chair. "Got it. Just downloaded it to the Simon server."

A miracle. "The window." I pushed it open and guided Cai through it, but Su hung back.

"I will stay here and try to keep them from chasing you."

"But they could arrest you."

She gripped my shoulders, then kissed my cheek. "I am a survivor. Go get your wife and daughter."

Out the window, Cai and I scrambled down the hill. I paused behind another rundown structure to look for MSS agents and check for updates from Simon. They'd just sent a text: *Verifying.*

"All good?" Cai asked.

"Hopefully. Let's keep going."

We continued our trek and reached the bottom of the hill unscathed. "I have a friend in the area. I will go to his place and be safe. Do you need to join me?" Cai asked.

My phone buzzed. When I read the text, elation filled my soul. "They told me congratulations. Thank you, Cai. You are amazing."

As Cai and I hugged, another text came in from Simon.

Walk to the black Suburban at the curb and get inside. Your family awaits your arrival.

I spotted the SUV and gave Cai a thumbs-up. As she walked off, I approached the car, trying to see the driver. Not surprisingly, his eyes were hidden under his hat.

I slipped into the backseat, and the doors locked. No sign of Anna or Maddie. I heard a hissing sound. Within seconds, I grew sleepy, woozy.

A damn trap.

I reached for the door and pulled at the handle. It was locked. I had no control of my limbs, no strength.

"Anna! Maddie!" I yelled.

And then everything went dark.

60

Unknown location

I awoke in a coughing fit. Instinctively, I tried to cover my mouth.

My arms didn't move. Neither did my legs.

I was on a table, zip-ties securing my wrists and ankles to metal bars.

A man appeared at my side.

"Who are you?" I blinked gunk from my eyes. The man was organizing metal instruments on a tray. He wore surgical scrubs, gloves, and a mask. *A surgeon ran Simon?*

"Where are my wife and daughter?"

He turned to me. "How are you feeling?"

"Where are Anna and Maddie? You said we'd all be free if I completed the mission. You have your code." My limbs pulled at the plastic restraints, biting into my skin.

"Yes, about that." He paused.

My gut churned like a hurricane in warm water. "About what? Why am I being restrained?"

"Your daughter is a wonderful little girl. She is doing well and is eager to see her father."

I stopped tugging on my restraints. I stopped breathing. I just stared at the man's eyes.

"Your wife had an unfortunate accident."

A tremor took hold of my body. I clenched my jaw shut to stop the chatter of my teeth. "An accident? Is she okay?"

"We were going to release her and Maddie. I wish she had just listened to her caregiver."

"What happened? Where is Anna? Was she injured?" The tremor swelled like a tsunami—nothing could stop it—and the edges of my heart began to crack.

"Your wife became paranoid that we were going to harm her and your daughter. She didn't listen to her caregiver. All she had to do was be patient."

"Where is she?" I jerked my head around—lights blazed in a stark-white room.

"Jack, she did not make it."

A sound emerged from my body. A sound I didn't recognize, but it had to be mine. A sound of unmitigated pain. Gasping for air, I thrashed and screamed. "I don't believe you! What did you do to her?"

The man grabbed an 8x10 photo and stuck it in my face. I stopped cold. Anna sprawled on the floor, her face a sickening blue. A single line of what looked like dried blood etched on her forehead. My beautiful Anna. The mother of my daughter. Gone. Murdered.

My body's tectonic plates shifted, generating a new eruption. Screaming, thrashing, cursing, crying.

"Jack!"

When I paused to breathe, I picked up a metallic scent. Blood from the plastic zip-ties cutting my wrists and ankles.

"This was an unfortunate incident. You will have your daughter. First, we have business to discuss."

Unfortunate accident? Business? All the emotion, every ounce of my being, converged into singular fireball, exploding with a force that could not be contained. My arms and legs broke through the restraints like they were made of tissue, and I pounced on the doctor. As I wrapped my fingers around his neck, he lunged for the table of metal instruments. The tray slammed to the tiled floor, and both of us followed. My shoulder took the brunt of the force, but I didn't release his neck. Red veins in his eyes grew more pronounced. I would watch him die. An eye for an eye. That was all that mattered. I would avenge Anna's death.

The surgeon swung an arm toward my face. I jerked my body to the left, and the scalpel took a chunk out of my shoulder. He slipped out of my grip and ran toward a door. He would not escape my wrath. As I jumped to my feet, I scooped up another scalpel. I caught up to him in three steps, slamming him into the door. When he bounced back in my direction, he swung his arm again. I was ready this time and blocked it, then I drove my blade into his neck and sliced downward.

His eyes bulged as he dropped back on his ass, his hands trying to plug a fountain of blood.

I was tackled to the floor by two men appearing out of the blue. A prick in my arm. I became drowsy, but I didn't fall asleep. Within seconds, I was back on the bed, four men holding me down—I was awake but with zero energy. Someone carried the dead surgeon out of the room and picked up all the metal instruments.

Two nurses appeared by my bed, and then another surgeon. I concluded that the first surgeon did not run Simon. Which meant this guy likely didn't either. They were disposable, just like my wife, apparently.

"You can have your daughter back."

"Maddie," I said softly, realizing my rage had nearly led to Maddie losing both parents. "Where is she?"

"In due time. You do want your daughter back, correct?"

"Of course. When?"

"There is one condition."

"What? No, no. You never told me about a condition. We were done. I did everything you fucking asked!"

Silence.

My brain sent off signals to launch into a new tirade, but the drug they'd injected into me blocked any action. "What now?"

"A trade. You for your daughter."

"Dammit," I said, my voice cracking. "You said you'd give her back."

No response.

"Okay, okay, I'll do whatever it takes to free her from you." I tried to imagine how this would work, who would take care of Maddie. But I was far too anxious for my brain to cooperate.

"You need to complete three more missions."

"That's the trade?"

"Mostly."

"There's more?"

"To trust that you will not run away from your responsibilities, you will have an electro-vial inserted into your body. The vial contains a small chip. If you abort your mission for any reason, a communication will be sent to that chip, releasing a concoction of drugs into your bloodstream. You will die within minutes. If you attempt to remove the electro-vial, it will be known, and the same command will be delivered."

This had to be Simon's plan all along. They had their code to the Chinese ICBM weapons systems, but it wasn't enough. They wanted more. To what end?

"I want to see my daughter first."

He ignored me. “After the procedure, you will be told where you can pick her up. You will have twenty-four hours to set up her care and her new life. Then you will be given the dossier on your next mission. If you fail to show up, there will be no second chances. The drugs will be released into your bloodstream and your daughter will lose her second parent.”

“I want to see her now.”

“After, Jack.”

The surgeon started to slip an oxygen mask onto my head, but I wiggled my head away from it. “Why are you doing this? I mean, you told me some story about my athletic prowess, and cooking books for the mobster, and how I’d do anything for my family. Other people must meet those criteria. Why Jack Whitfield?”

“It was easy. You came highly recommended.”

The oxygen mask was placed over my nose and mouth, and I inhaled despite myself.

61

Hong Kong International Airport

I cupped a hand over my eyes to fight against the glare as I scanned the road leading to the airport's international terminal. I was looking for the vehicle that would bring my daughter back to me at long last.

I heard a car door shut, and I spun to the right. Maddie, with Woofies in tow, was running right for me. A dimpled smile turned into tears as she leapt into my arms. She sobbed into my shoulder, unable to speak, and my heart began to crack anew. But I couldn't break down in front of her. She deserved the best of her father, the strongest parts of him.

That emotional transition started in earnest on the plane in the middle of a game of rock, paper, scissors. Maddie suddenly became catatonic. And so began the most difficult conversation of my life.

I rested my hand on her back. "Are you okay?"

She pulled her sights from the floor and looked at me with moist, brown eyes. "Mommy tried to save us. And when I ran out the door, I thought she was behind me. But I turned around and she wasn't there." Her little lip quivered. I brought her to me and held her tight.

She sniffled, then pulled back. "I went back and opened the door, and Mommy was on the floor, b-bleeding. Not m-moving." With each word, she became more worked up.

"Maddie, I wish I could—"

"She died, Daddy. She's never coming back."

As much as I wanted to shield Maddie from the pain, I couldn't hide the truth. "No, she's not."

"They killed her, right?"

I nodded and kept a gentle hand on her back. I told her that once she got settled with her Aunt Zeta, she would be able to talk to a counselor and it would help.

"Don't wanna talk to no one about it." She curled her little hands into fists, squeezing until her knuckles turned white, and then she turned to look out the window.

I gave her a couple of minutes, then leaned in close. Through breaks in the nighttime clouds, there was a sprinkle of lights from a city down below. And I thought of something that might help.

"Sparkling lights," I said.

She nodded. "I like sparkling lights."

"Just like your mother. She loved sparkling lights."

She gave me a side-glance. "I know. We're the same."

"Yes, you are. And every time you see sparkling lights, that's your mom looking at you and smiling."

She eyeballed me, looking skeptical but hopeful at the same time.

"Your mom will always be watching over you. Just like me. You will be safe, Maddie. I can promise you that."

Just before landing, I excused myself to the restroom, where I splashed water on my face and looked in the mirror. A quake took hold of my gut and didn't let go as my mind ran rampant with imaginary images of Anna murdered and my little girl screaming for her life. Unable to contain my rage, I hurled a fist into the mirror.

Shattered. Bloodied. Scar tissue—emotional and physical.

I would take that next step. For the memory of Anna. And for Maddie's life.

62

Dallas, Texas

I paused my stroll through the garden and observed two hummingbirds taking turns eating from the birdfeeder. When I was young, fascinated by the only known bird species that could fly backwards, I'd asked Mama if we could get a hummingbird feeder. Her response? "No money for that kind of foolishness."

Unless you were Zeta Ambrose, apparently.

I rounded the garden's third water fountain along the crushed gravel path that led to Zeta's lush backyard. Maddie was barefoot, blowing bubbles, giggling every time Zeta's little Australian Shepherd, named Spots, chased after the stream of bubbles. Aunt Z, as Anna had always called her, was busy blowing out her own bubbles, laughing and playing with Maddie as though she were a teen. But she was far from it, in fact.

"Hey, Daddy, come play with us." Maddie executed a pirouette, creating a funnel of bubbles for Spots to chase.

"You're very talented, Maddie." And she rushed over to give me a big squeeze.

"Aunt Z is too, Daddy. Don't forget her." Maddie giggled as she ran off, exposing her carved-pumpkin set of front teeth. She'd shown me another loose tooth on the plane ride from Hong Kong to Dallas. I'd already given Aunt Z a special treat to place under Maddie's pillow whenever the tooth fell out.

"You've got some pretty mad skills too, Aunt Z," I said.

She winked at me and continued playing with Maddie. I went back to my thoughts, mostly about how we'd gotten to this peaceful place so quickly.

Once Maddie was in my arms in Hong Kong, the first call I'd made was to my best friend back in Donelson. Daniel listened intently and didn't judge me or pepper me with a million questions, and I'm certain he had many. I gave him Zeta's name and explained at a high level what needed to happen in the next twenty-four hours. He only asked me one thing before he took action. "Why can't you take care of Maddie?"

I hated to do it, but I lied. I said my new career would force me to be on the road constantly, and I needed a stable, loving person to watch after Maddie. Not sure if he totally bought it, but he agreed to help.

Aunt Z was more than stable. Anna had once told me that her mother's stepsister had the kindest heart and sweetest disposition of any person she'd ever known. And it had always stuck with me.

I was most concerned about how Maddie would deal with the whirlwind reunion and handoff.

I snapped back to the present when I heard Maddie and Zeta in a fit of laughter over something Spots had done. Zeta showed her the perfect combination of kindness and playfulness. Just like a loving aunt would. Technically, she was a great-aunt. "North of sixty," she'd told me, but she wouldn't say how far north.

And so, as the afternoon gave way to dusk, I gradually sacrificed my alone time with Maddie so she could grow more comfortable with Aunt Z. It was difficult, but necessary.

Zeta had once been the top real estate agent in Dallas. Never married, no children. Retired for more than five years now, she'd said, "I've got more money than a third-world country. It's about time I use it for someone I love."

She promised to enroll Maddie at Hockaday, one of the most prestigious girls' private schools in the area. Most importantly, she would have Maddie see a child psychologist for the foreseeable future. I realized it might take a lifetime for Maddie to work through the trauma she had experienced. Zeta also said she would upgrade the security across her property. Cameras, lighting, even create a safe room inside. She then told me that she would spoil Maddie like never before.

That made me slightly uncomfortable, knowing how Anna and I had raised Maddie without relying on material things.

"If anyone deserves to be spoiled, Jack, it's your little girl. And the emphasis will be on love, listening to her and allowing her to feel safe."

Zeta had convinced me. I owed her so much.

The goodbyes to Maddie were relatively quick. She'd grown weary of the emotional breaks. A father knows. She felt safe with Aunt Z in her beautiful home, and especially with Spots.

"I don't know what's led to this, Jack," Aunt Z said to me at the front door. "And I know you can't tell me the real story. But you have my word that I will love that little girl with everything I have. You go do what you must to keep Maddie safe, and she will be here waiting for you when you're done."

My Simon-issued phone buzzed. I pulled it out of my pocket and looked at the screen. A text.

Do not be late for your flight. There is much to accomplish. You will need every ounce of strength and focus to be successful.

Just remember what is on the line.

I shoved the phone back in my pocket and watched Maddie chase Spots through the living room behind Zeta, her excited laughter filling me with overwhelming emotion. I fought back tears that had been threatening for hours, days even, and embraced Zeta with a fierceness that surprised me. And probably her too. I said I'd be in touch whenever it was possible.

And I walked away, already preparing myself for the second mission.

THE END

Forced into the hellish game orchestrated by the enigmatic figures who run Simon, Jack is quickly pulled into a world of illegal weapons, interactions with a brutal crime family, and a coup attempt on a neighboring country. But Jack is also drawn to helping two new friends. And then he must decide: will he sacrifice his own life to save others, or can he somehow complete the mission and rescue his friends? To follow Jack in his next riveting adventure, pick up NEVER SAY DIE.

Want a FREE short story about Jack's past life? Sign up for my Newsletter and receive a FREE short story. Eleven years before Jack's life is upended, he receives an offer he can't refuse—until he's directed to carry out an assassination. Is it a crazy nightmare, or has he somehow been activated by an outside force?

Click with this link to sign up for my Newsletter and get this free short story, *THE RECRUIT*:

https://www.johnwmefford.com/newsletter.html

John W. Mefford Bibliography

The Jack Whitfield Thrillers

BARRACUDA (Book 1)

NEVER SAY DIE (Book 2)

NOW OR NEVER (Book 3)

NEVER AGAIN (Book 4)

THE ENEMY WITHIN (Book 5)

THE HANGED MAN (Book 6)

THE CONDUCTOR (Book 7)

THE LAST DISCIPLE (Book 8)

The Alex Troutt Thrillers (Redemption Thriller Collection)

AT BAY (Book 1)

AT LARGE (Book 2)

AT ONCE (Book 3)

AT DAWN (Book 4)

AT DUSK (Book 5)

AT LAST (Book 6)

AT STAKE (Book 7)

AT ANY COST (Book 8)

BACK AT YOU (Book 9)

AT EVERY TURN (Book 10)

AT DEATH'S DOOR (Book 11)

AT FULL TILT (Book 12)

The Ivy Nash Thrillers (Redemption Thriller Collection)

IN DEFIANCE (Book 1)

IN PURSUIT (Book 2)

IN DOUBT (Book 3)

BREAK IN (Book 4)

IN CONTROL (Book 5)

IN THE END (Book 6)

The Ozzie Novak Thrillers (Redemption Thriller Collection)

ON EDGE (Book 1)

GAME ON (Book 2)

ON THE ROCKS (Book 3)

SHAME ON YOU (Book 4)

ON FIRE (Book 5)

ON THE RUN (Book 6)

The Ball & Chain Thrillers

MERCY (Book 1)

FEAR (Book 2)

BURY (Book 3)

LURE (Book 4)

PREY (Book 5)

VANISH (Book 6)

ESCAPE (Book 7)

TRAP (Book 8)

The Booker Thrillers

BOOKER – Streets of Mayhem (Book 1)

BOOKER – Tap That (Book 2)

BOOKER – Hate City (Book 3)

BOOKER – Blood Ring (Book 4)

BOOKER – No Más (Book 5)

BOOKER – Dead Heat (Book 6)

The Greed Thrillers

FATAL GREED (Book 1)

LETHAL GREED (Book 2)

WICKED GREED (Book 3)

GREED MANIFESTO (Book 4)

To stay updated on John's latest releases, visit:
JohnWMefford.com

Made in the USA
Coppell, TX
08 July 2025

51627000R00156